# A STERN LORD FOR MY LADY

## HER STERN HUSBAND - BOOK ONE

### R. R. VANE

Published by Blushing Books
An Imprint of
ABCD Graphics and Design, Inc.
A Virginia Corporation
977 Seminole Trail #233
Charlottesville, VA 22901

R. R. Vane
A Stern Lord for My Lady

eBook ISBN: 978-1-64563-968-8
Print ISBN: 978-1-64563-969-5
v1

# PROLOGUE

*T*he lady sniffed, her eyes now blurry with tears. Her bottom stung, but she didn't have the courage to rub it. She had tried to do so earlier, and that had earned her a second trip on her punisher's lap.

The lord who'd punished her studied her with a faint smile on his lips.

"You have only yourself to blame for it, my lady. I've only given you what you were asking for," he said.

The lady nodded, wiping her tears. He was right. Wasn't she fully responsible for this?

"Turn around and hoist your skirts," the lord knight said in a stern voice.

She widened her eyes at him. Hadn't he, only moments ago, straightened her skirts after the stinging spanking he'd delivered? She glanced at him warily, but he kept the same stern expression upon his face. She did not dare disobey him, so she did as he'd commanded, beginning to ask herself frantically if he meant to deliver further punishment on her bottom. Would he use something other than his hand now? Something that would sting even worse than the sound hand spanking he'd delivered?

Maybe that switch he'd cut from the apple tree in the yard, and which, she knew too well, lay in its corner by the door...

Her lord perused her at leisure. The lady didn't dare turn her head to look at him, but she knew his fine hazel eyes were glancing upon her bottom and upper thighs, which had been thoroughly spanked and must be a good shade of red. Moments passed, and she found herself holding her breath. Was he satisfied with the spanking he'd given her, or would he resolve he needed to spank her again?

"So, my lady," he said softly, after a while which seemed to her like an eternity. "Here we are now. You have certainly been spanked, but the question still remains, have you been spanked soundly enough?"

# CHAPTER 1

*London, 1172*
*Six weeks earlier*

*B*ertran FitzRolf stared at the letter he'd read so many times. It held disdainful words and phrases, which cut to the bone. It bore the De Lancres seal, but the one who'd dictated it had been, in fact, the lord's daughter, Lady Alicia, whose clerk had plainly written her name on top with a flourish. Lady Alicia began by thanking Bertran for his regard. The thanks were perfunctory. The lady then proceeded to give lengthy reasons for rejecting his suit. Chief among those reasons was that he was *naught but a lowly bastard*, unworthy of joining hands with a great heiress such as herself. There were other cutting phrases that referred to Bertran's lowly status, and to his being an upstart, who'd only recently gained royal favour through deceit.

Bertran heaved a deep sigh. He was more saddened than angered. These were grievous insults, but it was not the first time he'd been called a bastard. It was, indeed, what he'd been at the time of his birth, though his parents had not meant to make him so. In truth, they had been married at the time of his conception, but, as it had turned out, Bertran's mother's first husband, believed to have fallen in the Holy Land, had not been truly dead. He'd returned to claim his wife and had found her remarried to Bertran's father. The Church's position on the first marriage had been clear, and the new marriage annulled. At the time Bertran was born, his mother was no longer married to his father, but had gone back to her first husband, as the Church had decreed. And that first husband would never recognise another man's babe as a son of his blood.

Bertran tossed the letter on the table, casting a measuring glance at his parents, whose grim faces bespoke both sadness and anger. They'd never considered their firstborn son a true bastard. A mere year later, his mother's first husband had passed away, leaving her free to marry Bertran's father, the man she'd come to care for. His parents had gotten remarried, truly and properly this time, and then Bertran's two brothers and two sisters had been born. His father had petitioned the Church to rescind their ruling over Bertran's status, but it had taken years of tedious arguing and pleading, in order to remove the stigma of illegitimacy from his son's name. Bertran had by then gotten used to styling himself Bertran FitzRolf, rather than as Bertran de Morne, and had become accustomed to his position in life. He might have been his father's firstborn, but, as long as the Church had refused to acknowledge it, everyone else apart from his own family had regarded him as a child conceived in sin. Still, Bertran was now no longer considered a bastard. The Church had finally rescinded the former ruling and he was now a true De Morne. However, this seemed to make no difference to the proud Lady Alicia.

"The lady is presumptuous and vain," Bertran said gruffly,

gesturing to the letter. "But her words are not entirely deceitful. The prelates have since relented, but I was born a bastard."

"Don't ever say that!" his mother cried, with a look of deep anguish upon her face.

To this day, his parents were deeply grieved by what had occurred. Bertran had, in truth, not cared that most of his life he'd been called a bastard. *They* had, because they'd suffered and they'd felt it was unfair that their son should suffer unjustly. In truth, Bertran had never greatly suffered. He'd risen in royal favour through his own merit, and was now held in high esteem by King Henry. Even if brief, his first marriage had been to a woman of good birth and considerable property. And he'd recently attempted to contract a second marriage, to one of the wealthiest heiresses in the land, Lady Alicia de Lancres. But, obviously, Lady Alicia de Lancres thought him far beneath her.

"The insult shall not stand!" his father said grimly.

His parents had gone as far as to show Lady Alicia's venomous letter to King Henry, who'd proclaimed himself incensed by the discourteous treatment a mere woman had bestowed on his worthy vassal. Bertran smiled bitterly to himself, knowing that what had incensed King Henry had not been the disdainful way the lady had rejected his suit, but the fact that Lady Alicia de Lancres aimed to marry another, Lord de Jarnac's son, Sir Erec. Lord de Jarnac's lands were vast, and they bordered those held by the De Lancres family. If such a marriage were to occur, the De Jarnac family was sure to rise in power and prominence. Certainly, King Henry did not want it so. He did not want one of his vassals to hold that much wealth and power. Especially not since things were going so badly between him and Queen Eleanor. And especially since the whole of Christendom had been appalled by the king's order to kill Thomas Becket. The king felt under threat, and a De Lancres marriage to a De Jarnac would be a threat. Bertran and his family were unwittingly caught in the king's game.

"The lady will be made to wed you. The king will force her to do so by royal decree. And he will have her pay for the insults she's delivered," his mother said, with a set look on her face.

Bertran sighed.

"Mother, I no longer wish to wed her. It's plain she holds me in contempt. I do not wish to wed a woman who holds me in such ill regard!"

He'd tried to argue with his family, but they seemed set on their course. They had taken true offence at what the lady had written, and they'd enlisted royal support to set things to rights. He could argue all he pleased that he would not wed a woman who thought him unworthy of her. His family and the king had already decided otherwise.

"Nevertheless, you'll wed her," his mother said in an indomitable voice. "You'll wed her after you punish her in front of the court for all to see. They shall all see such an insult to our family will not stand. And they shall all see my son is well able to handle a haughty, wilful wife who thinks herself above him."

At his family's behest, the king had also decreed a punishment for Lady Alicia, for her lack of propriety and for the affront she'd brought to his vassal. The wedding was to be preceded by a humiliating spanking, in front of all the assembled court who would thus have occasion to see what happened to women who thought themselves above all authority. This humiliation was, undoubtedly, also intended for Lord de Lancres, who, for a while now, had seemed to favour Queen Eleanor's plight. But the spanking would be borne by his daughter, who'd shown herself presumptuous and wilful. And now, as her future husband, meant to rule over her, Bertran himself was called upon to deliver this spanking.

"I do not wish to spank her!" Bertran called in vexation.

He didn't wish to spank Lady Alicia, and he didn't wish to marry her. In fact, he wanted nothing more to do with her. She had rejected his suit, although, formally, it should have been her father, not the lady herself, who had final say in the marriage. Still, she'd rejected his suit. Ungraciously so. Bertran wanted nothing more to do with such a woman. The set look on both his parents' faces however renewed his conviction they would not relent.

"She deserves to be punished!" his mother said, looking pointedly at the letter.

Bertran nodded. Here, he could not but agree with his mother. Aye, the lady fully deserved a punishment, not for her rejection of him, but for her arrogant words.

"The king told me he'd have ordered a flogging, if she hadn't been a woman and of high birth," his father said.

Bertran frowned. The king was quick to dispense punishments, wasn't he? Everyone recalled only too well the penance that Henry had been forced to withstand in front of everyone, for the killing of Thomas Becket. The king had accepted to be publicly flogged, as penance for what he'd done. So now he seemed more inclined to humiliate others in a like manner, because the former humiliation must still chafe.

"But there'll be no flogging. Just a well-earned spanking," his father went on. "This is certainly a mild punishment, given the venomous, hurtful things this woman has written about a lord the king holds in high favour. I daresay her pride will be bruised far worse than her bottom."

"I do not wish to spank her!" Bertran repeated, in irritation. "Can't her own father spank her? It will be more appropriate!"

"You are to be her husband, and she's insulted *you*. You should be the one to mete out the punishment!" his mother said pointedly.

Bertran raked a hand through his brown hair. His first wife had been a meek, gentle woman. She'd been a dutiful wife, and had never given him any grief. He'd mourned her sincerely when she'd passed away, three years ago, due to a fever caused by a miscarriage. He was now almost six and twenty, childless, and in need of a new wife. When his mother had suggested a match with Lady Alicia de Lancres, he'd been somewhat surprised. The lady was above him in wealth, and he'd only recently risen in rank, due to his services to the king. But when King Henry himself had called upon him, suggesting the same match, Bertran had known he'd have to offer his hand to the lady, since it was not only his family's ambition, but his monarch's wish he should do so. So he had written to Lady Alicia's father, not fully expecting his marriage proposal to be considered. The lady was already twenty and still unmarried. It was rumoured she ruled her father's estates with an iron fist, and wished to continue to do so. And it was also rumoured she ruled her father. People said she was wilful, arrogant and haughty. And Bertran had not felt very keen on such a wife. Still, he'd been a dutiful son and vassal, and had attempted to enter marriage negotiations, just as he'd been advised.

"Why would you wish such a woman upon me? A woman who despises me and who's sure to give me grief?" he asked his parents bitterly. "Do you care so much for her lands and dowry?"

His father shrugged, muttering, "Still, her estates and dowry are not to be overlooked. She is perhaps the wealthiest heiress in the land…"

His mother sighed, coming to touch his shoulder.

"You know," she said with a smile, "Matilda of Flanders, King William's wife. You know the rumour that goes about the way they got married?"

Bertran shook his head. Queen Matilda was a paragon of female virtue. Why was his mother bringing her up at this time?

"Rumour goes," Bertran's mother went on, "at first, Matilda rejected William's suit, on account of him being a bastard. A lowly bastard, she called him, unfit to marry a high-born lady such as herself."

Bertran widened his eyes. He had not known this tale.

"And do you know what William did? He came to call upon

her, then took her upon his knee and gave her a good spanking in front of everyone to see. A humiliating public spanking…"

Now Bertran could see where his mother was going. Everyone knew William and Matilda's marriage had been highly successful, with both spouses genuinely fond of one another. He frowned. His mother was wrong to assume, just because Matilda had made the Conqueror a good wife, Lady Alicia would prove the same.

"Word goes William stormed into Matilda's father's castle and whipped her bare behind with a strap, until she, mightily sobbing, took back every single insult she'd uttered against him," his father added. "And it certainly taught the lady a lesson. She graciously apologised, and accepted William's suit with a teary, tremulous smile, the chroniclers say. She had, after all, just come to perceive his mettle, and she could already tell he'd make her a worthy husband. No woman truly wants a man who meekly accepts her insults. So there's no better cure for haughtiness than the one William provided for Matilda. And you'll administer a similar cure to Lady Alicia."

Bertran looked at both his parents, in deep annoyance. They seemed to take it as fact that he would relish making a spectacle of himself and of the woman who'd rejected him. He didn't. He relished privacy, and he didn't share his parents' ambitions. He glanced at them pensively, understanding he could, after all, afford to defy them. He was not dependent upon his parents' estates, having come into property of his own. So he could stand against them. They would be grieved, but they cared for him enough and would ultimately bow to his wishes. But there were not only his parents to consider. There was also King Henry. If Bertran opposed the marriage, the king could assume that Bertran wished to rally with Queen Eleanor. And Bertran knew it would be a mistake. He'd sworn fealty to his king, and he meant to be loyal. Due to Lady Alicia's foolish behaviour, there seemed to be no turning back from this marriage.

"I'll have to spank her, if I marry her, for all to see," he muttered grimly, knowing his parents had a point. Lady Alicia had insulted him in the worst possible manner.

He would bring shame upon his noble house if he married the lady without making it plain he would not stand for her insults. Besides, the king had already decreed the punishment. The lady's fate was sealed and Bertran would only be carrying out an inevitable sentence. He reasoned now it would be better for her and less harsh if *he* were to spank her, and not one of the king's appointed henchmen. He would only spank to teach her a good lesson, not in order to provide a cruel spectacle.

Both his parents seemed relieved by his reluctant assent.

"It may not be such a hardship," his father told him, with a smile. "After all, you were married for more than two years, and I'm sure you remember how to discipline a woman," he added, ignoring the sudden glare his wife cast in his direction.

Bertran nodded, in some embarrassment, and deftly steered the conversation to other matters, regarding the marriage contract. He felt deep relief when his parents were finally gone, leaving him alone to ponder on what he had to do. He'd not given the truth to his father. He did not remember how to discipline a woman. He'd never disciplined his first wife. She had been a sweet-tempered woman, so she'd never given him cause to do so. But the lady he was about to marry was not a sweet-tempered woman, was she? Now sighing in earnest, Bertran recalled he'd upon occasion heard his friends talk about the discipline they bestowed on their women. He conjured these occasions in his mind, deciding to use them as examples that would help him conduct himself appropriately. They seemed instructive as to the spanking needed to provide an adequate punishment for Lady Alicia.

# CHAPTER 2

$\mathcal{L}$ ady Alicia straightened the dress she wore, a new cramoisy gown, trying to appear calm and confident. Both she and her father had been summoned by King Henry to Court. A mere formality, her father had assured her, before Alicia's betrothal to Erec de Jarnac would become final. Alicia had accompanied her father with misgivings. She'd come to perceive King Henry was not favourably disposed towards her father or their family. Henry was always looking for ways to fill his own treasury, and his coffers seemed perpetually empty. He did not like it when his vassals possessed wealth, and he did not like that Alicia's father was in favour of Queen Eleanor and her eldest son by the English King, Young Henry, who, for a while now, had been at odds with his father. While not openly supporting Eleanor and Young Henry, Alicia's father had nevertheless given to understand that he approved of the queen's feuding with her royal husband. Alicia herself did not care for all this. She cared for her marriage to Erec de Jarnac, which was agreeable to her. Sir Erec was amiable and courteous, and he would prove a biddable husband. Besides, he was wealthy and well born, wealthier and better born than Bertran FitzRolf, whose suit she'd rejected. Still, FitzRolf and his family held the king's favour. Would Henry be angry for her rejection of FitzRolf?

Alicia made her curtsy to the sovereigns, both seated on their thrones. Eleanor was newly returned from her own court in Poitiers, and would remain in England only for the marriage of her son, Young Henry, which was to take place in August. Everyone knew Eleanor and the king were now barely able to sit in the same room together. Soon, Alicia knew, they might plunge the country into civil war due to their feuding.

"We have called upon you, Lady Alicia, to answer for the letter you sent to one of my most esteemed vassals, Bertran Fitz-Rolf, who's a De Morne."

Alicia held her breath. So, she had not been mistaken, Henry was displeased she'd refused FitzRolf. She looked to Queen Eleanor, pleading for her interference, but the queen cast her a stony look. Alicia felt a cold stab in her heart. So Eleanor could and would do nothing to help, in spite of the fact Alicia's father was loyal to the queen and her cause.

Suppressing a deep sigh, Alicia straightened her back, answering the king in a firm, but respectful voice.

"My father has refused FitzRolf's suit. It was his right to do so, my liege, since he did not consider this lord knight a suitable match for me."

Henry might still be their king, but he had no right to force his vassals to marry people of his own choosing. Besides, her father had rejected FitzRolf's suit graciously and courteously, so there was nothing the king could reproach them for.

"It has come to our attention, Lady Alicia, that *you* have shown disdain to the suitor you rejected, calling him *naught but a lowly bastard*," the king said, and it seemed his voice was angry.

Eleanor said nothing. She just stared away from Alicia in a displeased manner.

"There is a letter you sent to FitzRolf," the king continued.

"There were many other insults written there, which I will not read to the assembly, out of sheer respect for Sir Bertran and his family."

Alicia's heart went still. The king was plainly stating she'd rejected FitzRolf on account of him being a bastard. Alicia glanced upon her father, stunned. She'd not rejected Sir Bertran because he was a bastard. She'd rejected him because her other suitor had seemed a more appropriate match.

"Your father tells us he tried to prevent you from acting in such a discourteous, defiant manner, but it was to no avail. You've become a law unto yourself, a presumptuous, unruly female, who would not even obey her own father," the king continued.

Alicia could not believe her ears. It was a lie! Had her father said such a thing to the king? But why? She widened her eyes at the assembly, then cast a mystified look in her father's direction.

"Your arrogance and disobedience should be punished, daughter," her father said, not daring to look her in the eye.

She stared at him. The decision to reject Bertran FitzRolf's suit had been made of common agreement. She'd told her father Sir Erec de Jarnac was a better match, as his lands were bordering their own, and he'd readily agreed, knowing it was a wise choice. As was proper, his had been the clerk to pen the letter to send to Bertran FitzRolf, and she'd trusted the rejection her father had sent had been firm, but decorous. What kind of letter had her father dictated to his clerk?

Alicia now saw the whole court was watching her in deep silence, and she perceived Bertran FitzRolf's father, Lord de Morne stared at her with a stony look in his eyes. The king nodded to his vassal, giving him permission to address her.

"My son may choose to style himself FitzRolf, but he is a son I fully acknowledge. My firstborn. The son you disdainfully referred to as a lowly bastard," Lord de Morne said sharply. "The insult shall not stand!"

The faces of all those assembled were grim. Alicia took a deep breath as Lord de Morne tossed a letter at her feet. It bore her father's seal, but Alicia now painfully understood the insults had been written in her name. She pursed her lips and closed her fists, to prevent herself from berating her father. She'd always known he was a soft, mild man, but she'd never believed him cowardly. She knew he'd been offended by what he'd called the De Mornes' presumptuousness in asking for his only daughter's hand in marriage. She understood he'd used her as a shield behind which to hide in order to mock their presumptuousness.

King Henry did not look amused, and neither did the formidable Queen Eleanor. It was said that even she held Bertran FitzRolf in high favour, although she was now at odds with her husband. Alicia scanned the assembly, trying to figure out who among the assembled lord knights was Sir Bertran. He should be standing close to his father's side. Would he be wearing the De Morne house colours, which she knew to be white and blue? Her gaze was drawn by a tall knight standing on Lord de Morne's left. He had a big, tall frame, which was broad-shouldered. His hair was light brown and his countenance somewhat rugged. And he was staring at her. She found it hard to hold the stare of that pair of grim hazel eyes with gold flecks in them. He was not wearing the De Morne house colours, but a simple, unadorned tunic of brown-green. However, by the way he was staring at her, there was no doubt left in Alicia's mind. This was Bertran FitzRolf, the suitor she'd rejected. She perused him, unable to stop herself. A lean, narrow waist and a tall frame. Incredibly broad shoulders and arresting eyes. A countenance that seemed enhanced, rather than marred, by that faint, white, vertical scar which slashed the side of his left cheek, and extended to his forehead. Dispassionately, she decided he was a better-looking man than even Sir Erec. But that did not make him a better match for her.

King Henry spoke, and it was with deep anger when he did so.

"The insult shall not stand. But the marriage will stand. By royal decree."

Alicia looked at the king, mouth agape. He could not do that, could he? She shot a look of alarm at her father, who hung his head.

"Besides, De Lancres has already rescinded his former rejection and has now given his consent. Haven't you, De Lancres?"

Her father nodded, speaking in a hollow voice.

"Yes, my liege. Yes, I have."

Alicia could not believe her ears. Was her father truly so cowardly? Hadn't he had the courage to tell her of what had passed? He usually discussed each and every decision with her, so why not this one? Glancing at him, she understood he felt ashamed that he had to bow his head and accept the king's command. And she also understood he'd rather place all the blame on his seemingly wilful daughter, rather than fully acknowledge his own shame. Queen Eleanor did not seem inclined to help, so her father had to bow to Henry's rule.

"The insult should not stand though," Lady de Morne uttered, echoing the former words that had been spoken, and coming to stand by her son's side. She was a tall, distinguished woman whom Alicia had sometimes glimpsed when she'd been at Court. Lady de Morne cast a disdainful glance in her direction.

"And it will not, my lady De Morne," Queen Eleanor spoke at last, bowing her head in acknowledgement. "My royal husband and I will see the punishment carried out, by your son, in front of the whole assembled court."

Punishment? Alicia told herself this was one of those nightmares from which she was going to wake up soon, safe in bed, in the solar at her home. Still, the murmurs of assent from the crowd sounded very real to her ears.

"Lady Alicia, since I've decreed FitzRolf should be your husband, it's only fair he should be given the chance to school you to better manners, before the wedding vows are made and the contract is signed. A woman's obedience is her most prized virtue. And I will have my vassal marry an obedient woman," King Henry said with a faint smile on his lips.

Alicia stared at her sovereign, not knowing whether to speak and truly uncomprehending what was going on. She knew she'd unwittingly given grievous offence to the suitor she'd rejected, and it was plain the king had also taken offence. But, she understood in some relief, the king did not think to banish her or imprison her in a convent. Instead, he'd decreed that she marry FitzRolf. Was that her only punishment? What more punishment was her royal liege speaking of?

"You may proceed, Sir Bertran," the king spoke, nodding in the direction of the tall knight she'd perceived.

With widened eyes, she watched the tall knight approach her, then firmly take hold of her hand. She glanced at her father helplessly, as the knight dragged her to him. Her father had folded his arms, and was making no gesture to help her. Indignation rose high within Alicia, and she found her voice, shouting, as she began to struggle, "Wait! I demand to know what's happening!"

There were guffaws from the assembly, and a voice in the crowd saying derisively, "You'll know, my lady, soon enough."

Alicia belatedly saw that Sir Bertran was dragging her towards a wooden bench, which seemed to have been placed apurpose on one side of the dais where the royal thrones stood. How had she failed to notice it before? She'd been too distraught, obviously. She widened her eyes in horror when she saw what lay upon it. Unmistakeably, she recognized a willow switch, long and supple.

"What Sir Bertran will do shall be a lesson to all ladies who act discourteously to worthy lord knights who've earned the royal favour," the king's voice intoned.

There was no doubt in Alicia's mind as to the nature of her punishment. Rage and humiliation burnt inside her, but she understood it was to no avail to scream or keep struggling. It would only make the humiliation worse. So she stopped struggling. She braced herself to be valiant, thinking the ordeal should soon pass. She'd close her eyes through it and brace herself through the pain. And then it would all be over.

She strived not to protest when her captor placed her, face down, over his lap, positioning her for her punishment and firmly pinning her arm behind her back. But he seemed to hesitate for a moment, and the king's voice came to spur him.

"Through her own arrogance, the lady has forfeited all right to modesty, Sir Bertran. You're to deliver a punishment that is memorable for all those present."

It seemed to Alicia that Sir Bertran heaved a soft sigh before he lifted her skirts, displaying her bare bottom for all the court to see. Alicia felt she would simply die of shame, but, thankfully, only her bottom was on display, as her quim was modestly hidden by her position over his knee. Still, there was no modesty in the way her front lay pressed against this man's body.

"Proceed, Sir Bertran," King Henry's voice boomed, with grim satisfaction in his voice.

Alicia braced herself for the sting of the switch across her flesh, but the switch didn't come. Instead, a large hand made a slapping contact with the centre of her upturned bottom. She heard the loud spank at the same time as she felt its unexpected sting. Her face blazed with shame, and with the realisation she was feeling a young, handsome man's hand against her skin, in this intimate, undignified position. She thought to herself that the switch would have been preferable. It would have stung more, but it would have spared her the added humiliation of this intimate contact.

She stared at the red-carpeted dais, unable to close her eyes. The second spank that soon landed, in the very same spot, simply burnt, and she just did not have time to catch her breath as a volley of further, rapid spanks fell across her heated bottom cheeks. The fiend who was delivering them had a large hand, like a shovel, and it easily covered the most vulnerable parts of her bottom. Alicia winced and bit hard into her lip every time the fiend's hand made contact with her bottom. Both cheeks. Left cheek. Right cheek. Both cheeks again. Merciless spanks that spared nothing. They were setting ablaze every inch of her upturned rump. Soon Alicia lost count, and she began to buck and wriggle under the sheer scorching fire of the punishing hand. Yet the fiend's other hand seemed to have an iron grip, and held her firmly in place.

The spanking seemed to go on forever, bringing scalding tears into her eyes and a nearly unbearable, infernal heat in her bottom. The fiend appeared to know well what he was doing, since his main target tended to be her sensitive sit spots. The pain was becoming too much to bear, and Alicia found herself first crying, then simply blubbering, not caring who would hear and see her absolute humiliation. She just wanted him to stop. She even opened her mouth to entreat him to do it, and beg forgiveness for everything the court thought she'd done. But it seemed to her she'd even forgotten how to speak. So she only sobbed, in pain and utter shame.

The fiend stopped, just at the moment she'd thought he never would. She just lay there, sobbing, too weak to even wriggle, as his firm left hand still held her in place. His right hand now rested on her bottom, and even the touch of it was too painful to bear.

Through the haze of her tears, she heard King Henry's merciless voice.

"You've yet to use the switch, Sir Bertran," the monarch said.

Alicia sobbed, incredulously. The sting was already unbearable. Now the switch would surely make her swoon with pain. Yet she didn't dare ask for mercy. It would be cowardly of her to do so, and even more shaming than the punishment she'd undergone.

Sir Bertran's hand still rested on her bottom, and at last he spoke, in a gruff voice that sounded strangely soothing.

"Enough, my liege. I say the lady's had enough."

The unseen crowd around them seemed to be buzzing with gleeful zest and laughter, but at this point Alicia did not truly care for them. She felt a wave of unbounded gratitude for the fiend who'd spanked her. He seemed more merciful than the king, although he'd put this mighty burn into her bottom. The burn was fierce, but, at this moment, as he was resting his big hand on her scorched skin, she felt an unexpected pang of pleasure inside her quim. A sweet, delicious ache that blinded her to everyone around her. At this moment, the crowd seemed to have dissolved around them, and there seemed to be just her, lying across his lap, feeling his palm against her tender flesh. The way his palm was resting upon her seared skin kindled a strange sort of fire inside her, as if the blazing sensation in her chastised behind had conquered her entire body. She recalled only too well how comely the fiend was, and how she'd struggled to tell herself this did not matter when she'd first set eyes on him. Yet she also recalled the king was now glancing upon them, and she recalled the switch hadn't been yet employed. Would the king still command Sir Bertran to use it?

BERTRAN SUPPRESSED A SIGH, feeling a stab of pity for the sobbing woman who lay on his lap. He'd spanked her hard, and her bottom was now a shade of fiery red, nearly matching the dress she wore. No doubt she'd have trouble sitting down today, and the sting may extend even tomorrow. Yet, he'd not spanked to bruise, putting more sting than sheer thumping force into his spanks. She was sore and uncomfortable, but not in numbing, mindless pain. He was a solider, but not a brute, and he was smart enough to realise he'd share his life with this woman. He knew she already despised him, and was well aware she would be furious with him for what he'd done, in front of everyone to see. Yet, there was still a chance she might not hate him. He'd only chastened her. Very well so, indeed, and she seemed spent and subdued. Adding further pain to an already blazing bottom would be an unnecessary cruelty. And it may make her hate him. There was no point in earning his future wife's hatred. It was enough he already had her disdain.

From where he sat, King Henry cast him a displeased look, but Bertran didn't flinch, holding the monarch's stare. Bertran might be the king's vassal, but he was now a lord held in high esteem. So he would heed his king's command, but speak his mind when he thought it was his right to do so. Lady Alicia was to be his wife, and as her almost husband, he had the right to discipline her as he saw fit. At this moment, Bertran deemed the discipline he'd bestowed on his lady was enough. He was aware the king would enjoy a further spectacle, one that involved a good switching, but he was not inclined to provide such entertainment for the king. It was shaming enough for both himself and his future wife that they'd had to conduct this lesson in discipline in public.

Queen Eleanor whispered in her husband's ear, and the king heaved a deep sigh.

"Very well, Sir Bertran," he said rather reluctantly. "We can all see the lady's well and duly chastened."

The murmurs from the crowd seemed somewhat disappointed, and Sir Bertran glared at those lords and knights who were avidly looking upon his future wife's shapely, well-rounded bottom. He deeply resented their avid stares, but a part of him could not fault them. As it was, he was having a hard time controlling his arousal, and had been struggling to do so throughout the whole punishment. He'd never spanked before, nor had he thought his cock might wish to stir while he was doing it, but Lady Alicia's bottom was a true wonder to behold and touch. Firm and rounded just to his liking. He loved the scorching heat of it under his palm, and he found himself loving its freshly spanked redness. It looked simply delicious.

He was aware she was still sobbing softly, as she lay in her undignified position, and he felt very guilty for his enjoyment of the punishment. He was indeed aroused by the intimacy of the punishment they'd shared, yet he did not truly take pleasure in her discomfort. He also knew he'd humiliated her in front of the entire court, and, to a proud woman like Lady Alicia, the humiliation must burn ten times worse than the spanking itself. He hadn't failed but notice she had not begged for mercy or forgiveness. She was proud, and, he had to admit, valiant, even in her defiance. He'd known grown men, soldiers, who didn't display as much restraint and dignity when they took their punishment.

He gently lowered and straightened her skirts, covering her bottom, and noting she sobbed even harder as he did so. He'd been often spanked in his childhood, so he knew too well the kind of pain she was experiencing now. He felt sorry for her, as he helped her stand up. He saw her wince in pain, and cover her bottom with both hands, rubbing it furiously for a moment. Then he saw her become fully aware of the crowd simpering behind her. Lady Alicia gritted her teeth, and suddenly let go of her bottom, straightening herself and squaring her shoulders, in a regal gesture. She had dignity, that much was plain, and he couldn't help but admire the way she now faced the crowd, head held high, as she calmly wiped her tear-stained face with the kerchief she'd pulled from her sleeve.

"Let this be a lesson to all haughty, presumptuous wives," King Henry said, rising, obviously meaning this jab for Queen Eleanor who was at strife with her royal husband.

Queen Eleanor smiled brilliantly, apparently oblivious at her husband's jab. Bertran had always privately thought she was twice the ruler her husband was, but the king was his liege, and it was to him he would always offer his loyalty first.

"Now, since the dire part of this day is over, let us get on with the merry part of it. An exchange of vows, followed by a wedding feast, which Lord de Lancres has been kind enough to provide at his own expense," Eleanor said graciously.

De Lancres nodded, rather green in the face. Bertran knew only too well he'd been coerced into funding a lavish wedding feast for his daughter at Court, which Henry had demanded of him. Bertran himself did not particularly look forward to the feast. He despised crowds and court entertainments. But he supposed he would have to suffer through all of it. He cast a sideways glance at Lady Alicia, who was standing by his side, dejected, but straight as an arrow. *She* would certainly have to suffer through all of it. Even if he knew her punishment was well deserved, he felt sorry for her, especially since he knew she would have to suffer one more humiliation this night. She would have to lie with him, a bastard she despised.

Honour decreed he should breach her maidenhead tonight, allowing for the sheets to be displayed as proof of his bride's virginity. He didn't put it past Lady Alicia to seek an annulment if he did not do the deed tonight. She might try to seek shelter in a convent if the marriage was not consummated, claiming her husband was in truth unable to claim his rights. Bertran could never shame his family thus. The taint of bastardy that had clung to him so long had shamed them enough.

Truly not knowing how to act around a woman he'd just spanked, Bertran awkwardly offered Lady Alicia his arm. She glared at him, but, to his relief, she reluctantly took it. They proceeded to what was to follow.

# CHAPTER 3

The rest of what happened took place in a sort of daze. Alicia's bottom was blazing when she watched her father sign the marriage contract. And it still smarted, somewhat less fiercely, as Sir Bertran presented her with a wedding gift, as tradition decreed. Alicia felt like laughing, bitterly – he'd already gifted her with a stinging, crimson behind, so any other gifts now looked ridiculous. Still, she forced herself to accept his gift, wordlessly, with a gracious incline of her head. She was not addle-brained, and she understood too well that wails, tears or protests would serve to naught now. There was a royal decree, and her marriage would take place, whether she acquiesced or not. Besides, she had no doubt that the fiend, Sir Bertran, would not hesitate to take her over his knee again, for a new lesson in humility, if she dared protest. She ruefully glanced at his large right hand, noting, in impotent fury, that its palm was still somewhat reddened by the exertion he'd made when he'd spanked her. She fervently prayed that his hand felt at least an ounce of the burn that her own bottom was keenly feeling right now.

On her finger, the groom slipped a ring with both their initials carved on it, as was proper. He pinned the gift he'd bestowed on her gown. It was a conventional gift – a ruby brooch, a symbol of fidelity. As the blessings and the vows were exchanged, Alicia sat through all of it like a martyr, striving not to fidget from one foot to the other, to take her mind off the soreness in her bottom.

A serious issue presented itself later, when the newlyweds were supposed to seat themselves in their honour seats, beside their sovereigns, at the king's high table on the dais. Ribald laughter and jokes assailed Alicia's ears as she hesitated in front of the seat she was supposed to take, even after a page brought a red cushion for her comfort. Both the lords and the ladies assembled found great merriment in her hesitation, declaring loudly that the cushion looked as red as her spanked behind must still be. Both monarchs found equal entertainment in it, and the jest continued, as Alicia sat silent, blushing crimson. It was uncomfortable to sit down, but possible. She didn't spare a single glance in her father's direction. She felt sickened by his cowardly behaviour, and certain her deep humiliation could have been spared if he had been truthful with her.

She gritted her teeth, and she braced herself to bear a wedding feast that was proving to be far more humiliating than any other thing she'd had to suffer. It was not how she'd ever pictured her wedding. A wedding was an occasion of joy and honour. She strived not to hang her head in utter shame, and stared at the trencher in front of her. She and Sir Bertran shared a knife, trencher and goblet, and she noted he'd already cut a choice morsel of venison, which he was offering to her. He was behaving graciously, as a courteous bridegroom should, when only hours before he'd spanked her hard to make her pay for the insult he'd received.

She shook her head mutely. Tonight, she lacked all appetite.

"You should eat something, my lady," he told her in a deep voice.

It was only the third time she'd heard him speak, and she

vividly recalled she'd been lying across his lap, bare-assed, when she'd heard him speak first. Deep heat crept into her cheeks, as she shook her head again. She struggled to meet his gaze, lest he should think her a coward, but, in truth, she still felt deeply shamed by what had occurred between them. And she felt deeply shamed as that ignoble, treacherous fire ignited inside her sex when she looked upon his face. He was comely – perhaps not handsome according to all the canons of male beauty, but comely nevertheless, his comeliness strangely enhanced by the faint white scar slashing his left cheek, and by those arresting eyes, which were not blue or green or dark, but hazel and gold-flecked.

The jokes and laughter around them rang harshly in her ears. Some of the guests were still making fun of her well spanked bottom and of the future chastisements her husband might have in store for her. Others were merrily bringing up the wedding night she and her lord would spend together, a wedding night that promised to be fiery indeed, in view of what had occurred. Sir Bertran didn't seem any more amused by the general merriment than she was. He just sat through all of it with a rather grim expression on his face, eating calmly. She noted he drank sparingly. She decided to take a sip of wine, and felt somewhat restored by it.

He perused her with his gold-flecked eyes.

"You should not drink on an empty belly," he cautioned her gruffly, extending a new morsel of meat to her. She frowned at him, already disliking the way he was presuming to command her. Sir Erec would have made a biddable, genial husband, and he'd have suited her fierce disposition better. This man was not the right choice, even if he stirred that treacherous, lusty heat inside her. Alicia wondered what could be wrong with her, to moon over a man vain enough to want to humiliate her in front of everyone to see.

She shook her head.

"I cannot bear food right now," she said, making her meaning plain by casting him a disdainful stare.

She'd been wrong to believe him merciful for sparing her the switch. Wasn't he the one who'd demanded she be punished in full view of everyone, in order to pay for the insult? And wasn't he the one whose ambition had spurred him to covet her dowry? He was certainly arrogant and vain. And she suspected he'd spared her the switch just in order to make a show of his magnanimity in front of the court. She harboured no illusions, however. He would make good use of it in the future. He was not a compliant, biddable husband, but one who would demand blind obedience. And Alicia knew herself not to be an obedient, meek woman. She had a temper, and she had no doubt he'd try to bring her to heel. She had been right to reject his suit. They were simply not right for one another.

He raised his eyebrows at her, and Alicia calmly wondered if he'd make her pay for her effrontery later. No matter. It would be just one more, painful humiliation to add to the one she'd undergone earlier. She pictured her future life, and she didn't like what she envisaged.

"As you wish, my lady," he told her, turning away from her, and taking a sip from the goblet they shared.

Soon it was time for the bedding and Bertran braced himself for the full, tedious, ribald ceremony. He bore the jokes of those who attended to his undressing, and who helped him into a fur-lined robe, and waited patiently for the time when he should join his bride in the bedchamber that had been readied and blessed for the wedding night. He strived hard to plaster an eager smile on his face, as he let his laughing attendants lead him to the bedchamber when it was announced that the bride was ready for the bedding. He strived to smile so no one would perceive his doubt and anguish. He'd punished the lady, and he feared she would prove unwilling to share the bed with him. Yet the deed had to be done tonight. Bertran prayed fervently that the lady would prove herself willing.

Once he'd been brought to the bedchamber, he observed Lady Alicia was fully naked, with only the curtain of her luscious chestnut hair to shield her. As custom decreed, the ladies who had helped her undress now raised her thick long hair to reveal her naked body in all its glory. Large, overripe breasts with pink nipples that looked like rosebuds, pleasantly rounded hips and shapely thighs. In her dress, Lady Alicia had looked attractive, but in her nakedness she looked simply beautiful. He should have expected it. Hadn't he glanced upon her naked bottom and found it simply wonderful to behold?

The ladies bid Lady Alicia to turn round for her groom to look for blemishes, but there were none he could see. He held his breath noticing her naked, luscious bottom, still glowing red from the spanking he'd delivered earlier. There was more laughter and teasing from those gathered to witness the bedding, but he turned a deaf ear to it all, unable to take his eyes off his new bride. She might have been unwilling. She might disdain him. She might be furious at him for what he'd done, but, at this moment, he found he didn't care for any of it. He simply wanted her.

He stood patiently while his own attendants got him out of the robe he now wore, parading him naked in front of everyone to see including his bride, who should in her turn be able to spot any blemishes that might be there. He nearly blushed as he felt her green gaze on him. It was a bold gaze that seemed to be taking in everything there was to see. There were his battle scars, of course, but these counted as honourable tokens, and not as blemishes. And there was his cock, which was now standing to full attention in front of her, oblivious to the gawkers who were crowding the bedchamber.

27

There was more laughter, and ribald jokes that alluded to the groom's eagerness.

"Oh, my," one of the older ladies attending said, with a knowing laugh. "My lady Alicia, you might have been right to reject this one. He's clearly prone to impale you mightily. I do not know if you'll survive this night."

Bertran found himself scowling at the woman, knowing her ribald comment would only make things worse. His bride was already furious with him. There was no need to add fear to the fury....

When finally, the onlookers were satisfied with the fun they had at the newlyweds' expense, they left, allowing Bertran and his new bride their privacy. Bertran stared at his bride awkwardly, picking up his discarded robe and closing it over his nakedness. He wanted to proceed slowly. He meant to be gentle in his lovemaking and mindful of Lady Alicia's innocence, because he knew no other way. It would be dishonourable to behave otherwise.

He noted she made no effort to conceal her own nakedness. His cock throbbed painfully, but he restrained himself. He looked at the tray that held a pitcher of wine and goblets, and wanted to offer her some of the wine, but he recalled she'd eaten nothing.

"So, my lady, at last we are alone," he said artlessly.

She gave a bitter laugh, and he noted she was still standing by the bed. Certainly, she still found it difficult to sit down on the sore bottom he'd given her. He opened his mouth to tell her the public spanking hadn't been his wish, but the cold look in her green eyes stopped him short. There was deep disdain mirrored there. The anger he'd felt towards her those weeks ago, when he'd first read her letter, came back in full force. She had insulted his family grievously, and now she didn't seem to show any sign of contrition, not even after the painful lesson he'd delivered. What was he ever going to do with a wife such as she?

His first wife had been meek and gentle, not haughty and defiant as Lady Alicia certainly was.

He heaved a sigh, striving to keep his temper. It was their wedding night, and he had every intention of keeping both his lust and his temper well in leash.

He stared at her, not knowing what to tell her to make her despise him less. He was not a man of many words, and he was not schooled in flowery phrases or honeyed talk. So he simply didn't know what to tell her.

"Wife, I should call you *wife* now, my lady…" he muttered, searching his brain for something he might say to her.

She cast him a bitter smile.

"You can call me whatever you please, my lord. You've made it clear you want me for your chattel. So – here I am. Your chattel. To do with as you wish."

He nearly flinched at the coldness in her words. She went on in the same disdainful, mocking voice.

"I'd lie on the bed with my legs spread for you, if I could, in order to submit as a good wife should, but since you saw fit to chastise my bottom soundly, I find myself unable to do such. I've seen beasts couple though, dogs and horses, and since men are not so different from beasts, I can guess the position would be right for coupling."

He widened his eyes at her as she went to prop her elbows on the bed, thrusting her bottom to him and offering him a perfect view, not only of her well spanked behind, but of her pink quim.

"I reckon it is coupling you have in mind, my lord. So, here I am," she said, in a mocking voice. "You can mount me if you wish."

Deep lust blazed inside him, and he barely contained his impulse of doing just as she asked, thrusting inside her roughly from behind. But there was also fierce anger mingled with lust. She was adding further insult to the ones she'd previously bestowed upon him. It was more than plain she was mocking him.

"I see now I was wrong to spare the switch," he found himself snarling in irritation.

"You are within your rights to use it now," she countered calmly, still maintaining the position that had become maddening to him.

It was a lovely view – the red, lush bottom she was thrusting towards him, and the pink sex he craved.

He willed himself to be calm, weighing what he should do next. She didn't seem to fear the switch, although, he knew, if he were to fetch one and use it, he'd reduce her to sobbing in a matter of moments, as her bottom was still tender from the spanking she'd received in the Hall. Certainly, he could do so, but that wouldn't change things between them. She'd resent him even more, and, at this moment, in spite of his anger with her, he found he didn't wish her to resent him. He lusted for her, and he wanted her to welcome him inside her.

He frowned upon her well spanked bottom. The position she'd adopted might, after all, provide a solution to his conundrum.

"I've spanked you well, my lady," he said, knowing a proud woman like her would find his words humiliating. "But maybe not well enough…" he added softly. "It's best I test for myself if my handiwork will suffice or if you need more."

In spite of his earlier irritation, he had no intention of spanking her again tonight. She'd had enough, and she'd been through enough. Still, that didn't mean he couldn't use his earlier spanking to bring her where he wanted.

Without giving her time to change position, he came behind her and gently placed his hand on her reddened behind. It was warm to the touch.

"Nice and warm. I've done a thorough job of it, it seems," he told her lightly, as he caressed her tender cheeks.

It was at that moment she moaned. Bertran frowned. Was that a gasp of pain or a true moan of longing? It had sounded like a true moan of longing to him, but maybe his ears had deceived him. He softly caressed the crown of her reddened buttocks, and there it was again, that moan, which sounded very much like longing.

"Just stop," she told him in a strained voice.

"Are you in so much pain?" Bertran asked in some concern.

It was the first spanking he'd delivered, after all. And, in spite of his care not to use his full strength, he might have been too harsh in disciplining his new wife.

"Nnn…Yes," she replied.

Bertran didn't miss her hesitation though. A slow smile curved his lips as he bestowed another, feather-light caress on her rounded buttocks.

This time she took a deep breath, stirring a little under his touch. His smile broadened, as he realised they might not be as ill-matched as he'd thought at first. He'd been aroused by the spanking he'd delivered, while she seemed to have become aroused by the spanking she'd received. But maybe it was so with all healthy males and females – there'd been a strange intimacy in the punishment. A kind of sharing, in spite of the public place he'd done it in. So maybe it was no wonder they were both aroused – he'd held and touched her already, even if not for caressing, but for chastisement. Still, it had been holding and touching. He knew himself not to be ill favoured, and he'd perceived her green gaze on the length of him when they'd undressed him for the bedding. She might protest, but it was becoming plain to him she was not as indifferent to this coupling as she'd proclaimed herself to be.

"Are you a maiden?" he asked her bluntly, now burning to touch her in that even sweeter spot between her legs, just to see if her sex was wet and eager for him already.

She gave an outraged gasp, yet she didn't leave her position.

"I've never dishonoured myself!" she told him in a dignified voice.

At this moment, Bertran would truly not have cared for her state. He wanted her too fiercely, and already knew he would have this marriage stand. His king and his family wanted the match. And he was already taken with the bride, despite her arrogance.

He sighed, now gently turning her to face him. If she was a maiden, then he should be mindful of her innocence.

"Since it is your first time, it would be unseemly to couple thus," he told her in a patient voice, gazing into her wide green eyes which no longer looked defiant but slightly anguished. "If I thrust inside you from behind, I would tear through and cause you more pain than necessary. It is not something I wish."

She widened her eyes at him.

"Isn't it? You seemed not to care about the pain you caused me in the Hall. In fact, I'm certain you rejoiced in it!" she told him in a voice laced with anger.

He sighed.

"That was a punishment. Our wedding night should not be a punishment for you," he told her.

ALICIA DEBATED WITHIN HERSELF, trying hard to keep her head clear. Oh, the fiend was comely, and she hadn't failed to notice his proud cock when they'd undressed him. She was a wicked, sinful woman for certain, because the moment she'd glanced upon it, she'd wished it inside her. What a vile, depraved creature she was! And when he'd shamefully touched her spanked bottom, she'd nearly swooned with the rapture of mingled pleasure and pain.

She narrowed her eyes at the fiend. He seemed sincere in his desire to be gracious to her when he claimed his husbandly rights. And she knew there'd be no return from this. It was either this marriage or the prospect of a bleak convent, since the king had been angered enough. Eleanor did not seem inclined to protect her, and Alicia very much doubted the king would allow her to make another match if there was an annulment of this one. She'd always longed to cradle babes in her arms, so the convent was not something she wished. Besides, she saw herself as a creature who took healthy pleasure in worldly things, not in holy endeavours. A convent life would not suit her at all. It would have to be the fiend then, though she knew she'd have no easy life with a husband set on chastising her at all turns to make her mind him.

She heaved her own deep sigh, in response to the one Sir Bertran had heaved earlier.

"Fine," she found herself muttering. "This night need not be a punishment for either of us."

He smiled at her and she stared at him in astonishment. It was the first time he was doing so, and she nearly melted under that smile. He was even more comely when he smiled, the beast. He looked upon her with his hazel eyes.

"I'm glad you see reason. And I'll be certain to find great enjoyment in our coupling. You're very comely, wife, but I'm sure you already know that," he told her softly.

She harrumphed. She supposed her looks were tolerable enough, but she'd never considered herself comely, not like the fair, blue-eyed ladies with their delicate, graceful demeanour and manners. And he'd be wrong to think he'd be able to subdue her into a meek, docile woman who swooned at the first sign of hardship.

"Let us dispense with honeyed words," she told him, recalling he'd not shown her any sweetness when she'd lain defenceless across his lap. "There is no need of such between us."

He gave her an appraising look, as his hand slowly began to

caress the contour of her cheek. Like earlier, she felt surprised a man who'd spanked her so hard could be so gentle.

"You're still not happy with our match," he said, as his fingers were caressing her, now sliding down the sensitive side of her neck.

She laughed incredulously.

"You've humiliated me in front of everyone! They'll talk of it for years to come! Lady Alicia's blazing red bottom! And you're asking me if I'm unhappy with the match?"

He shrugged, and she held her breath as his hand slid lower, slowly descending and moving away the long tresses of hair that were covering her left breast. Alicia had been too incensed to care for modesty, but now she keenly recalled she was standing stark naked in front of him, and she belatedly blushed. Fiercely.

"I reckon bruised pride and a sore bottom can heal after all. Don't you?" he eventually said, as he began to caress her nipple. The heel of his palm moved in circles, brushing it until it became a hard, aroused pebble.

She felt a deep stab of pleasure inside her quim, akin to the sweet ache she'd experienced when he'd caressed her bottom. She didn't answer him, too stunned with the way she was acting around this man. Like a true wanton. No wonder he'd asked her if she was still a maiden. Her behaviour was certainly brazen.

"I think it's time for a kiss, my lady," he said in the same soft voice, and he didn't wait for her acquiescence, capturing her lips with his.

There was a wonderful, wet breathlessness to the kiss she just loved, as much as she loved the feel of his body pressed against hers. But, after a while, she found herself craving more. Since he was still clad in his fur-lined robe and she was stark naked, she broke the kiss, reaching for the cord of his robe.

"You're bold, wife," he muttered, cocking an eyebrow at her.

She shrugged, reconciling the fact she was indeed brazen. But it had never been in her nature to be shy. She'd shouldered the burden of a big estate since a young age with little help from her father. There'd been no room for shyness or hesitation.

She untied the cord of the robe and stared at his long, aroused cock. Because she was a maiden, her father had not allowed her to help in the bathing of their male guests, so she was not familiar with the male body. But she'd heard the whispered comments in the bedchamber during the bedding ceremony, and she'd had occasion to see for herself. The fiend was well favoured, that was certain. His long cock was now prodding at her belly, stiff and hard, and she couldn't help it. She touched it lightly. It stirred.

He took a deep breath, then captured her lips hungrily, pulling her to him. His robe was entirely discarded during their embrace and she had the satisfaction of pressing herself against the bare, hard muscle of his body.

He broke the kiss, drawing away from her and raking a hand through his brown hair.

"Oh, wife, I think you'll be the undoing of me," he whispered.

He then lowered her on the bed, and she whimpered as he did so. Her bottom was still sore, and it was still painful to lie down on it. She glared at him, recalling he was responsible for it, yet that shameful, ignoble ache took hold of her nether parts. She was now gushing wet.

"Just raise your hips," he told her, coming above her, to prop himself on his haunches. "It will be less painful."

She frowned at him, but did as he bid her. She raised her hips trying to keep her bottom from plopping against the bed. His right hand came between them, and he touched her shamelessly between her legs. She moaned deeply, as his fingers found her sticky wetness.

"*Jesu*, you're gushing wet already…" he muttered, and it seemed to her he was incredulous.

She blushed, now knowing for certain he thought her a wanton woman.

He took hold of her hips, and she abandoned all modesty as she felt his hard cock brush against her slick entrance.

"Will you impale me now?" she asked him rather breathlessly, recalling the ribald joke one of the guests had made.

She supposed she should feel afraid. Instead, she felt her heart thumping and her sex even slicker with moisture.

"Oh, I will, wife. I will," he said in a laboured voice, and he swiftly embedded himself inside her, tearing through the barrier of her maidenhead.

There was pain, and for a moment that pain burnt fiercely, but, truth be told, it was less than the burn she'd felt in her bottom when he'd spanked her. He remained embedded within her, kissing away a tear of pain that had run down the corner of her eye.

"It will go away. Soon," he whispered soothingly.

He was proved right. The pain was indeed soon replaced by a pleasurable ache, and she found herself raising her hips to meet his thrusts as he began to slide in and out of her. Her sore bottom made her arch her back and meet the rhythm of his thrusts, and she soon noted the fiend perceived this and began to touch her bottom so she'd raise her hips to him as he thrust in. She suppressed a curse on her lips seized by both pleasure and pain. The fiend was making use of the sting of the spanking he'd delivered, in order to increase his pleasure in coupling. Yet Alicia came to understand he was not only increasing his pleasure but also her own. Soon she forgot to resent him, and the pain in her bottom was utterly forgotten as the throb in her quim became rapture. So much rapture. Alicia had never felt so, not even when she'd shamelessly touched herself between her legs in her bedchamber. Yet she knew the rapture for what it was. It was heavenly bliss. And as she shouted her unrestrained joy, she saw the fiend bestow his comely smile upon her. Kissing her lips ardently, he began to thrust inside her faster and deeper, then came to spend his sticky seed.

When she was able to come back to herself, Alicia attempted to glare at him, as he was lying by her side, spent, still smiling his comely smile. Yet she understood the fiend had not used her ill. Instead, he'd been mindful of her innocence and had given her pleasure. He'd bedded her well and had behaved honourably.

After she'd cleaned herself between her legs, Alicia lay beside her new husband, on her belly, feeling exhaustion soon taking its toll. This day had proved the worst day of her life. Yet... she began to doze off, dimly thinking this bedding had been the most pleasurable thing of her life. How could such a foul day feel so fair at the same time?

# CHAPTER 4

*L*ady Alicia had already fallen asleep on her belly, with her bare bottom still a delicious shade of deep pink. Bertran frowned a little upon this wife of his, so bold and eager, though she'd been just a maiden. He took hold of a blanket and covered her, loath to hide her wondrous body, but knowing that the royal residence could get chilly, especially at night, even if it was May. He lay beside her, but sleep would not come, and he thought with a smile of how well his bride's wet sheath had accommodated him. She was fiery and bold, this new wife of his, unlike his first wife, who'd been shy and skittish.

He recalled his first wedding night. It had been far removed from the one he'd experienced tonight. His first wife had been obedient, and willing to do her duty, but it had taken much work from him to get her eager and ready for his first thrust. Even later in their marriage, it had taken considerable coaxing and patience to get her to welcome him between her thighs. This did not happen often – she'd been devout and held all the holy days, which required them to abstain from coupling. Bertran had been barely twenty at the time, and he'd keenly craved frequent coupling. He'd been loyal to his wife though, because he held his honour very dear, and would not break faith with his lady, but sometimes his wife's austere behaviour had been a trial to him.

He smiled to himself, thinking his second wife could not have been more dissimilar from his first even if he'd wished it. Where his first wife had been sweet and meek, this woman was defiant and haughty. And where his first wife had been shy and restrained, this woman was bold and fiery. She'd ignited like fire, and he'd not even had the chance to caress her as he'd planned. He'd meant to pleasure her with his fingers and mouth, and make her gush and writhe for him in rapture before he took her, but in the end he'd had no need of doing it. She'd been already gushing for him, and, in truth, he'd only begun caressing her. She was a woman who ignited like tinder, this new wife of his.

Again, he smiled, only to have this smile replaced by a frown. If Lady Alicia ignited like tinder for him, what guarantee did he have that she would not do so for other men? She disdained him and what he was – her venomous letter had been more than clear in this respect. Yet, she'd coupled with him boldly. He fell asleep belatedly, with a crease on his forehead, not knowing if he should rejoice in finding a wife who ignited like fire under his touch or bemoan the fact that he'd found a fierce, bold woman who unashamedly revelled in coupling.

She was still asleep when he woke up next morning, with his cock stiff and ready, as it usually was when he roused. He sighed with regret, knowing he would not be able to avail himself of his lady this morning. She must be still sore between her thighs from last night, since he'd taken her maidenhead, and he didn't want to use her ill. So he pleasured himself, looking at her as she slept peacefully, and thinking of her scrumptious, reddened behind, which must be still somewhat pink from the spanking he'd bestowed upon her yesterday. He made quick work of it, because he was already very much aroused. He wiped the seed that had spurted from his cock with the bed sheets, which were already soiled from their coupling last night. There was some blood on them, but not much. She had been slick and eager, and this had eased his passage. Besides, he already suspected she'd sheathe him better than his first wife. He'd not given her his full length last night, mindful she was still tight and unused to a man between her thighs. But he already had an inkling this woman would be able to take his full length, to the hilt, the next time they coupled.

He watched her while she slept, still torn between joy and anguish. Last night, she'd plainly stated she hadn't wanted the match, and he assumed she still disdained him, in spite of the fact she'd given herself to him. Would she be loyal to him, to a man she obviously thought little of? He didn't know. He meant to treat her fair, and be a good husband to her, but would she try to be a good wife in return? She plainly hadn't learnt her lesson from the humiliating spanking he'd delivered. Did this mean he'd have to spank her even harder when she defied him? And he felt sure she would defy him again. She was not a meek, obedient woman.

ALICIA WOKE up with a pleasurable feeling inside her sex. She'd dreamt delicious dreams last night. She'd dreamt of her new husband, thrusting inside her, and then she'd dreamt of his hand, bestowing playful, but stinging spanks on her bottom. She opened her eyes, noting there was a slight discomfort in her behind, but not as much as she'd experienced last night. There was also a discomfort between her thighs, but she dismissed it, understanding it was natural for a newly deflowered maiden to feel thus.

She glanced upon her husband who was fully dressed, and noted he had not waited upon her to assist him. As his wife this was now one of her duties, but he didn't seem to mind dressing without assistance.

"Good morrow, wife," he said, perusing her with his hazel eyes.

She'd never thought she'd find hazel eyes so compelling. She'd always been partial to eyes that were blue, or green, but Sir Bertran's eyes were simply arresting. It was probably because of those gold flecks in them.

"Good morrow, my lord," she replied, now blushing in earnest.

She was unused to rising late, and it was remiss of her to wake up after her lord husband. Her mother had schooled her well, and she knew her wifely duties. Wives should never wake up later than their husbands, her late lady mother had decreed. What time was it? Well past dawn, for certain. Alicia had seldom woken past dawn, but she surmised it was the sheer exhaustion of the day before that had gotten to her.

"And how are you this morning, lady wife?" her husband asked her, coming to seat himself on the edge of the bed. "Still sore?"

Did he mean her bottom or that place between her thighs? She blushed even more fiercely than before when he pulled the blanket to stare at her upturned bottom.

"Still pink, I see, but not as angry red as yesterday," he said mischievously, giving her bottom a light pat.

She glared at him, though she'd not felt any pain, but rather an ignoble stab of pleasure in her sex at his touch. In truth, she'd even forgotten to feel angry with him for the burning, humiliating spanking he'd delivered. He had been courteous and gentle with her last night. But at the same time his loving had been pleasurable and hot. Perhaps she had been wrong – he might prove a tolerable husband, after all. And perhaps he'd really meant to spare her the humiliation of a painful switching in front of everyone. He'd only meant to make her pay for the insults her father had most certainly bestowed upon him. Replaying the scene in her mind, she reasoned he had been fair in the way he'd dealt with her. The insults the king had talked about were heinous – another lord knight might have asked payment in blood for such. Still, that didn't change the fact he'd humiliated her in front of the entire court, to satisfy his pride and ambition. They'd laugh at her for years to come – that was certain. She sighed, deciding to rise, knowing that, soon, the attendants would come to take the sheets away.

"Shall we leave this very morning?" she asked him, knowing this was a decision they should discuss. And if they left, where would they go? To one of his estates or to one of her own estates? Alicia knew her own estates were richer than those a De Morne would possess. So, choosing one of her manors as their chief residence seemed like a more reasonable choice.

He shook his head.

"No. I am needed at Court, so we'll stay for at least two more months or until I'm no longer needed."

She heaved a sigh, knowing he had to be present at Court, if his liege lord had decreed it. But that didn't mean she should be here with him, did it? She despised Court, and she felt out of place among the sycophantic courtiers. Besides, the whole court had witnessed her humiliation. She'd rather be elsewhere.

"It seems to me only *you* need to be at Court," she told him with a frown. "*I* can go to one of my estates, where I'm certainly needed."

She cast him a defiant look, daring him to set his boundaries. She already knew he'd spank her if she misbehaved. So, it was as good a time as any to test the limits of her new husband. Would he spank her for speaking her mind?

He heaved a heartfelt sigh.

"Queen Eleanor will be here until her son's wedding in August. She insists you should remain by my side, lady wife. Besides, we're newly wed."

He did not seem angry at her for her boldness, which was a

good sign. The fiend was maybe not as unreasonable as she'd thought him.

"I just despise Court," she said with a frown, deciding to test him further.

He raked a hand through his brown hair, and cast her a sympathetic smile.

"So do I, for that matter."

The fiend seemed reasonable, so far. And Alicia was not as unreasonable as to think they could go against a direct royal command.

"So, I guess we'll have to stay at the royal castle for the next two months," she said in a resigned voice.

He shook his head with a smile.

"No, not at all. I have a house in London, didn't you know?"

She hadn't, and she found herself smiling at him in relief. A place of her own would suit her fine, as the bedding in the palace would be uncomfortable and cramped. They'd only had use of this bedchamber because it had been their wedding night, but courtiers who remained at Court had to make their bed in the common space, with just a screenfold to separate them from the others who slept in the same room. The prospect of a house seemed mightily pleasing to Lady Alicia.

"When can I see the house?" she asked excitedly.

Again, her husband rewarded her with that smile which made him look impossibly handsome.

"Soon, wife. Today, after we've paid our respects to our lieges," he told her.

Alicia didn't have time to give her acquiescence. The servants, accompanied by two of the ladies who'd been present at the bedding ceremony last night, came to take away the sheets. One of the ladies, Lady Edith, the one who'd made the ribald joke about impaling, frowned upon the sheets as she was inspecting them.

"So little blood," she muttered waspishly, closely examining the sheets.

Alicia found herself blushing fiercely, as the lady in question glanced disdainfully upon her, as if she was calling her honour into question.

"More seed than blood," Lady Edith further commented, making Alicia blush even further.

She felt deeply embarrassed, since she knew too well the whole court would be still having fun at her expense.

"That would be all, my lady Edith," Sir Bertran said in a cold voice.

Lady Edith seemed to linger though.

"I'm bound to ask, since this is my duty," the elderly lady said, casting the new husband a shrewd glance. "Are you satisfied with the state of your bride, my lord?"

Alicia thought she would die of mortification.

"Aye, truly satisfied, my lady," Sir Bertran replied in clipped tones.

Mercifully, the lady Edith took the hint and soon made herself scarce, together with the others. Still, Alicia felt suddenly cross and despondent. She was no longer a maiden, but a married woman, and, as such, from now on, she would be subject to her husband's rule. The husband in question was eyeing her with a cocked eyebrow.

"Shouldn't you be getting dressed, wife?" he asked pointedly, gesturing at her nakedness.

Alicia had never been shy, and she'd forgotten her husband's gaze was upon her when the attendants had entered the room. Again, she blushed fiercely. Her late mother would be tossing in her grave. What could her husband be thinking of her, behaving so immodestly?

"Aye, my lord, it's high time I got dressed," she muttered.

She didn't call for attendance, and she proceeded to do so herself, under her husband's gaze. It seemed his hazel gaze was watching her every movement. Soon she began to feel aroused by the hungry way she perceived he was perusing her. Did he want to have her again? Alicia already knew herself to be willing - this man's gaze seemed to kindle a fire between her legs every time he looked upon her. She glanced at him uncertainly, not knowing what he would want of her. He was, of course, within his rights to claim her.

She looked upon him in plain disappointment when he at last told her he had court business to attend to this morning. They would meet later in the Hall, he told her, when it was time to see their monarchs.

# CHAPTER 5

*B*ertran spied the look of sheer astonishment that crossed his wife's face, as she glanced upon the dwelling they'd entered. His townhouse. It used to be a beautiful home, but since his first wife had passed, there'd been no one to oversee it properly. Embarrassment started to burn within him, as Lady Alicia began to inspect the chambers, noting their dusty and neglected state. In truth, now that he realised, the bedchamber, where he slept, was the only place in the whole house that was reasonably clean. The solar lay cluttered and unused, as for the kitchens she'd inspected earlier, they were in a sorry state indeed.

He breathed in sheer relief when his wife finally declared she had seen enough. Her inspection had been thorough, and the look written on her face was plain for everyone to read. She was not happy. Bertran braced himself for sharp words. She had all the rights to berate him for the state of his property.

"You do not spend much time at your London home, my lord," Lady Alicia spoke, and her voice was calm as she did so.

He smiled, rather sheepishly.

"In truth, I don't. During the day, I'm mostly at Court, and when I am at home, I spend most of the time in the yard, practicing with my men."

She nodded.

"I see."

She made no further comment to Sir Bertran's astonishment. He'd already perceived Lady Alicia was a haughty woman, and he'd expected she'd take this opportunity to show her further disdain of him. Besides, she was entitled to her rancour. The state of his house left much to be desired.

As it was early evening, they soon had their repast, and Bertran had further occasion to feel embarrassed by the shabby Hall and ill cooked, tepid meal they were served. He'd never paused to notice these things. As a soldier, he was not fussy about his meals, and always ate what was put before him, keeping his mind on the pressing business of the day. But he could see Lady Alicia was not used to such fare, and she ate but little, choosing instead to study her surroundings with keen green eyes. He could also see she chose to address his men, in a courteous, but firm manner, which left no doubt as to her station as the new lady of the house. She seemed at ease among them, as if she were used to being obeyed, and Sir Bertran began to realise that it was indeed so. Lady Alicia was a great heiress, and from what he'd heard, she, rather than her father, had held the reins of their vast estates. He was, in truth, beneath her, in wealth and rank, just as she'd stated in her letter of rejection.

He was still musing upon this even later, when time came to seek their bedchamber, and Lady Alicia had asked for a hot tub to be readied. He found she'd already entered her role as the lady of the house, effortlessly, as if she'd been long used to commanding his servants. And he noticed the servants already hurried to do her bidding.

When the tub was brought in, his lady wife dismissed the servants, readying to attend to him while he took his bath. She was behaving like a gracious wife, and he decided to be gracious in return.

"You should have your bath first, my lady," he told her, gesturing to the streaming tub.

She frowned at him.

"Husbands bathe first and wives attend to them. 'Tis custom," she told him.

He shrugged.

"I do not stand for ceremony. And I am used to tending to myself," he told her in earnest, watching as she widened her green eyes at him.

"You do not want me to attend to you then?" she asked, and it seemed to him her voice was displeased as she did so.

His cock gave a throb as she spoke the words, and he recalled how famished he was for her touch. Perhaps he had been hasty in refusing her gracious offer. He glanced at the steaming tub. It looked inviting and, come to think of it, big enough.

"We could attend to one another," he said softly, striding to where she was.

He cupped her face, claiming her lips for a kiss. For a woman who was haughty and defiant, his wife tasted truly sweet. He kissed her long and deep, taking his time to savour her full lips and to explore the hotness of her mouth with his tongue. She kissed him back, with the same abandon.

They undressed each other, and he noted with a smile that she was more adept at undressing a male than he was at undressing a female. In truth, he was unused to undressing women, as his wife had always done so herself, and the other women he'd coupled with during his widowed years had not required such assistance.

He studied his new wife with hungry eyes, as he began to lead her to the bathtub.

"Will it hold both of us?" she asked dubiously.

He helped her climb inside, pausing to glance at her luscious bottom as she did so. It was still pink, but only slightly so. He suppressed a small sigh, which felt strangely like disappointment, as he knew he would not have occasion to apply any discipline on this luscious bottom tonight. She had been gracious, and gracious wives deserved rewards rather than punishments.

He joined her, exhaling in pleasure at the hotness of the water, and unmindful that the tub was somewhat overfull.

"There's water dripping all over the floors!" his wife cautioned him, but he shushed her.

"No matter."

She frowned at him. "You seem unmindful of it, but the serving girls will have to clean the mess we're making."

She spoke reason, and he was not usually unmindful of those who attended to his needs, but tonight he felt like indulging himself.

"I promise to take better care in the future," he told her, as he sat himself comfortably in the tub, pulling her into his lap, so she was now straddling him.

"See," he added. "Now there's room enough for both of us."

Again she frowned, but he picked up the soap that lay beside the tub, and started tending to his bride. He could not resist, so he began with her full breasts, lathering them thoroughly. She was no longer frowning as he did so, and he just loved the look shining in her green eyes. There was a mixture of hot desire, puzzlement and innocence that he revelled in. Her rosy nipples had peaked, and, as he rinsed her breasts, he knew there was one more ministration he needed to add. He bent his head and took one delicious nipple into his mouth. She moaned, as he began to suckle it, his lips tingling pleasantly. After a while, time came to attend to the other parts of her, and he did so diligently, starting with her long hair, and saving her quim for last.

"Almost clean now, my lady," he told her after a blissful while. "Apart from your cunt."

He took pleasure in the way she blushed as he uttered the

word. Her cheeks might be blushing, but her full lips parted, and her green eyes shone with desire.

"It is a pretty little *chatte*. I should attend to it thoroughly," he said, lathering his hand, in order to make the entry of his fingers slick.

THE FIEND HAD CLEVER FINGERS, Alicia thought in a sort of a daze, as the fingers in question were kindling the fire between her legs. Soon, she abandoned all coherent thought, and let herself be carried by the way they slid in and out of her sheath. When she thought she'd swoon with joy, she knew his clever fingers had already found that part of her body, which brought her the most pleasure. Some went as far and called it the devil's teat, that secret part of a woman's sex, which was said to bring them indescribable delight. Was it sinful, what he was doing now? And would they have to do penance in Church for it? At this point, Alicia decided she'd worry about penance later. Pleasure was robbing her of all coherent thought. And it came crashing over her, like a wave. She peaked against his fingers, feeling her sheath pulse and clench in rapture.

She heard him curse softly under his breath, and found herself, once again, straddling him in the bathtub. He didn't wait, but just impaled her on his cock, grabbing her hips firmly, and beginning to pump inside her, hard, unmindful of all the water that was dripping on the floor. She braced her arms against his shoulders, keenly feeling the hard length of him as it slid in and out of her. There seemed to be more of him than there had been yester night. Even more hard length thrusting fiercely inside her. Soon, she forgot to ask herself why that was, and was seized by a new wave of bliss, and shouted her joy at the same time he spent himself inside her.

The water was lukewarm when she disentangled herself from

him. She frowned, understanding she'd been remiss in her wifely duties. She'd let her husband tend to her in her bath, and she hadn't tended to him.

"Just let me do your hair and back at least, husband," she muttered.

When he acquiesced, she did her duty to the best of her abilities from her position in the cramped tub, lathering his hair and soaping his back. There was a bucket of clear water by the tub, and she helped him rinse his hair, just as he'd done to her earlier.

"There, all done," she said at last, knowing they should get out of the tub, as the water was getting tepid.

"Good wives don't leave their husband's cocks unattended when they bathe," he told her with a smile, as his left hand was rubbing his eyes, to get them clear of water.

She stared at him.

"I thought I already attended to that," she muttered in puzzlement.

He chuckled.

"You're a new wife, so I'll be lenient tonight. You can further tend to it when we're both dry and warm."

He helped her stand up, and then got out of the tub, helping her out of it. Alicia looked mournfully at the wet floors, knowing that cleaning them thoroughly was another thing on the long list of household chores to add on the morrow. She would be busy setting this house to rights and directing the obviously unschooled servants to do what it took.

The fiend was as solicitous as ever, tenderly wrapping her in a dry towel, before he saw to his own drying. As he did so, she saw his long cock had gotten stiff again. She frowned. Had her late mother's lessons been remiss? Before her passing, when Alicia had been but fourteen, her mother had insisted on lecturing her on her marital obligations. Husbands' cocks were stiff when they needed to couple, and went limp after the coupling was done and their appetites assuaged. Did the stiffness in the fiend's cock mean she'd failed to assuage his appetite properly? Had he been right to chide her for her wifely neglect of him?

Once they were dry, Alicia went to put on her night shift. Her husband frowned upon her.

"Come here, wife," he commanded, extending a hand to her.

It was Alicia's turn to frown at him. So far he'd been gracious, but she disliked the tone of command in his voice. In truth, she was unused to being briskly ordered, and more used to commanding others in her employ.

She pretended not to hear him, and strode to lie on her side of the bed. He was free to come to her, if he wished more to do with her. He joined her, but there was a displeased crease on his brow as he did so.

Pulling her to him, so they were both lying on their sides, facing each other, he hoisted her nightgown to her hips, then proceeded to remove it altogether.

"Next time I tell you to come to me, my lady, I expect to be obeyed," he told her in a firm voice, which was, nevertheless, laced with teasing.

"What will you do if I do not, my lord?" she countered, feeling her temper rise. "Spank me? As you did in the Hall?"

His hand was now resting on her bottom, and Alicia drew in a sharp breath, understanding he now had full access to her bottom if he wished to apply chastisement on it. That treacherous ache settled inside her sex, and she wondered if the large hand that was now caressing her behind would see fit to redden it for her defiance.

For a moment it seemed he was preparing to do just that, but he did not. Alicia was astounded by the strange disappointment she felt.

"Perchance I should continue to be lenient tonight," he told her. "I am, in truth, a lenient husband, my lady, and mild-tempered," he went on, speaking softly. "Just have a care not to step too far out of boundaries."

He kissed her, without giving her a chance to reply, and she thought he would claim her again. But, after a while, he broke the kiss he'd been bestowing on her mouth, and began to kiss his way down to her belly. Alicia bit her lip in both puzzlement and delight. Her mother had never told her of this, or of the other things he'd done to her this night. Did all husbands behave such, or only hers? After a while, she found she did not truly care. He laid her on her back, and this time, there was no discomfort, as the pain in her bottom had fully subsided from yesterday.

The next thing he did, astonished her mightily. As he parted her legs wider, he bent his head and seemed to be inspecting her sex thoroughly. She blushed, knowing he was the only person who had ever looked upon her body thus.

"What are you doing, husband?" she asked, in full wonder.

"Just verifying if I tended to your cunt properly earlier, my lady," he countered with a smile in his voice. "It seems perhaps I didn't," he added in a playful voice.

And then he put his mouth on her, just like that. She started to protest, but she just couldn't find her voice to do so. What he was doing was certainly sinful, but Alicia readily reconciled herself with the sin of it. All creatures were sinful, and God's mercy was boundless. She surely felt He'd find forgiveness for this sin, just as He did for other sins.

She nearly swooned as her husband stuck his tongue inside her cleft. His tongue was just as clever as his fingers. And it just didn't content itself to tend to her now gushing opening. It teased her in that place of secret delight, until she peaked right against his mouth, blushing crimson at the thought of this wantonness the fiend was responsible of conjuring inside her.

When she came back to herself, she found him propped on an elbow, perusing her with a look of satisfaction upon his face.

"I've tended to you, wife, like a dutiful husband. Now it is your duty to tend to me," he said, lying on his back and tucking his arms under his head.

She widened her eyes, as she perceived his long cock, still proud and stiff. He couldn't mean she should put her mouth on him, could he?

BERTRAN LOOKED upon his wife through hooded eyes, thinking he might have been too forward. They were but newly wed and only last night he'd breached her maidenhead. But she was so bold and fiery, he kept forgetting how innocent she was. In truth, he'd never presumed to ask of his first wife this thing he was asking now. And, in truth, his first wife had not ever let him put his mouth against her own sex, even if he'd tried to coax her to do it. It was too sinful, she'd proclaimed, and he had known not to press for more, resigning himself to more restrained couplings. But this new wife was vastly different from his first, wasn't she?

He saw her weighing what he'd just uttered and he opened his mouth to set her at ease. He would not require it of her, if she did not feel like taking him in her mouth. She'd already given him great enjoyment, and there were many other, pleasurable things they could learn to enjoy together. But all thought was robbed from him as he felt her hand, at first hesitant, cup the length of him.

"Just tell me something, husband..." she said softly, as she began to stroke him tentatively.

He nodded, taking full pleasure in her soft touch, noting her hand was already beginning to get bolder.

"How come your cock is stiff anew?" she asked.

He glanced at her in some puzzlement.

"Why shouldn't it be stiff again?"

"But didn't you spend your seed earlier?" she queried, and her voice was earnest as she did so.

He chuckled, telling himself he kept forgetting she was new to coupling.

"Sometimes it's thus," he told her patiently. "Sometimes male desire is rekindled, even after lusty coupling. And the male craves coupling again."

Truly, her hand was getting bolder, and he bit into his lower lip, to prevent himself from spilling his seed too early and embarrassing himself. She weaved a powerful spell on him, this new wife of his.

"Oh, I see now… I just thought it must be something I did wrong," she told him, and her voice sounded filled with relief.

"No," he told her rather breathlessly. "It's something you did right. Right indeed."

Soon he was unable to speak, as she began to stroke him rhythmically, her earlier hesitation vanished as if through magic. He opened his mouth to tell her to stop, perceiving he was aroused beyond belief, but he did not have the chance. It was then that she lowered her sweet mouth and brushed a shy kiss on the tip of his shaft. His shaft pulsed dangerously, and a single drop of white liquid spurted from it. Bertran painfully gritted his teeth to prevent the rest from just spilling over. It was sweet torture, as her full lips began to suck the tip of him, then got bolder and hungrier. She was a fast learner, this new wife of his, Bertran thought, nearly maddened with rapture. He let her tend to him for a while, but stopped her just in time. He would not spill himself inside her mouth. It was too soon for such intimacy, and she might not enjoy it.

He disentangled himself from her, flipping her on her back unceremoniously and making short work of easing himself between her legs. He plunged himself into her slick wetness, to the hilt, loving the hot tightness of her. She would later feel sore perhaps, because she was still tight for a man of his size, but he possessed her with a powerful, breathless urgency, until they both came to shout their joy at the very same time. He then lay on his back, truly spent, realising that never in his life had he possessed a woman so fiercely. He looked upon her in some concern, now worried he'd been too forceful in his loving of her. However, he soon glimpsed a smile of contentment on her face.

"Good night then, husband," she muttered, snuggling against him, after she'd pulled the bedcover over both of them.

Never in his life had he been so ensorcelled by a woman, he thought with a frown. Was she as bewitched with him as he was with her? Or would she ignite as easily for any other man? Would she ignite more easily for a man she didn't despise? Again, he fell asleep with a mixed feeling of joy and discontent.

# CHAPTER 6

*H*er husband made a hurried departure on the morrow, to attend to the duties he'd been assigned at Court, leaving Alicia to accustom herself to her new dwelling. Queen Eleanor would be patient, he assured her, and would not require her presence until next week among her attendants. He'd told Alicia he would be tardy this night due to pressing matters and would thus also take his evening meal in the Royal Hall. He'd brushed a brief, hurried kiss upon her lips after he'd said so, looking upon her with hazel eyes which to Alicia had seemed filled with longing. But he'd hurried to his own chores, which left her the space to see to hers.

Entirely left to her own devices, Alicia didn't tarry to set to work, knowing that much needed to be done to set the place to rights. After she'd instructed the servants for the day, she proceeded to make a thorough inventory of the state of the house, noting those items in need of repair or replacement. Inspecting the furnishings, she concluded that a carpenter should be soon employed, together with a blacksmith, whose presence was necessary to see to the replacing of rusty hinges and locks. In truth, Alicia was looking forward to the busy months ahead of her, since they were going to be filled mainly with housewifery. It was a welcome break from the many tedious responsibilities she'd shouldered as mistress of her father's household, and as overseer of their vast properties. This time in London would provide a welcome respite from her many duties, and she'd be better rested when the time came she rejoined one of her country estates.

She knew by heart the properties that were part of her dowry, which now belonged to her husband, as well as the lands and manors she'd inherited from her mother, which were still hers by right, since they'd never been part of the dowry due to her husband. One of these days, she should talk on all of this with Sir Bertran, and inquire after his own properties, which, she already knew, were not as vast as hers.

She only stopped her work at noon, for a hurried repast, and was ready to get back to her chores, when news reached her that a visitor had come upon her. Lady Marguerite de Morne, her husband's lady mother. Alicia received her guest in full embarrassment, keenly aware of the sorry state of her new home. Besides, she couldn't help but recall it had been Lady Marguerite who'd clamoured for her punishment most fiercely. Her husband's mother must still resent her greatly.

Lady Marguerite heaved a deep sigh, as she looked around the house where the servants were busying themselves scrubbing and polishing, at Lady Alicia's behest.

"I've often asked my son to let me set this place to rights, but he'd always postponed it, knowing I had several other duties to attend to."

Lady Alicia nodded, aware that Lady Marguerite had not only the care of her own household and estates upon her shoulders, but also two other grown, unmarried sons and two growing daughters to see to.

"But now that he's wed, I suppose this burden falls upon your shoulders," the lady went on, casting Alicia an appraising look.

When she'd glanced upon Alicia in the Hall, there had been disdain in Marguerite's gaze, but now Alicia saw with relief that the lady was looking upon her with benevolence. Alicia felt shamed by it, recalling the insults to her son, which had been written in the letter. It was not she who'd insulted the lady and her family, but she felt fully responsible for the insult her father had bestowed.

She bowed her head.

"I pray forgiveness for the grievous insult you received, my lady Marguerite," she said formally.

Lady Marguerite touched her shoulder.

"You have already paid for it, so I should say all is forgiven and forgotten," she said with a smile.

She then added, looking at Alicia intently. "I was the one who insisted upon the match. Not mainly for your dowry, as you think, but because I knew of you, and because I still thought you'd make my son a worthy wife, in spite of your arrogant rejection of him. You were wrong to reject him. He will be a good husband to you, far better than that Erec de Jarnac."

Alicia said nothing, but mused there was some truth in what Lady Marguerite was saying. It was plain, in the bedchamber, Sir Bertran was a mightily pleasing match for her. Still, a marriage did not unfold only in the bedchamber.

"Perhaps there's something I should tell you," Lady Marguerite said. "It was not my son who insisted upon your public chastisement. In fact, he was loath to deliver it. We and our royal liege prevailed upon him, knowing honour had to be served, and the punishment we clamoured for was mild, compared to the insult we'd received."

Lady Marguerite was soon gone, since she and her family would leave on this very day to rejoin their demesne, but not before instructing Lady Alicia where she could engage the services of a good carpenter and of a reputed master blacksmith.

Soon, Lady Alicia decided to go on these errands herself,

instead of sending her people, since she suddenly felt the need of an outing. Lady Marguerite's words had caused turmoil inside her. So, her new husband had been against her public humiliation, which meant he was not as harsh as she'd believed him to be. Perhaps he had been speaking the truth to her, and he was indeed mild-tempered. Hadn't he proved himself so ever since they'd spoken their vows?

She went about her errands, pausing to enjoy the busyness of the crowded town of London and beginning to feel her spirits lift. She was able to employ the services of Master Levens, the carpenter, who would come to inspect their place on the morrow. She then proceeded to search for Master Reed, reputed to be the best smith in town, who lodged further away.

When she finally knocked on the smith's door, she was met by an apprentice boy, who told her that Master Reed was at his forge, at the back of the house, engaged in a portentous endeavour. The boy smirked as he directed her to where his master was, and Alicia and the serving man accompanying her looked at each other in some puzzlement. But as soon as she set eyes on where Master Reed was, she had cause to widen her eyes.

With astounded eyes, Alicia instantly understood why the boy had smirked knowingly in their direction when he'd spoken of his master's doings. At present, Master Reed was in the yard of his forge, holding a sobbing woman across his lap, while he was brandishing a willow switch, not quite unlike the one Sir Bertran had spared Alicia from, the day of her punishment. The woman's skirts were hoisted, and her bare bottom and thighs were already striped with red. By the zest with which the master smith was still brandishing the switch, more red stripes were bound to appear on his wife's upturned rump. The stripes now looked angry red against the skin of the woman's well-rounded bottom. Master Reed was handling the instrument of his punishment with full vigour, and Alicia guessed this harsh chastisement was nowhere near done. She felt a stab of deep sympathy for the sobbing woman, as well as some measure of strange excitement in witnessing this event. She glanced sideways at the serving man who'd accompanied her and saw a look of avid wonder on his face. Ashamed of herself, she averted her eyes and turned to leave, vowing to come back later, when Master Reed was less occupied. But, at that moment, the smith raised his eyes and paused with the switch in mid-air.

"My lady, pray have patience. I shall attend to you immediately, after I am done attending to my wife. There is a seat yonder, you can rest for a bit until I'm done."

Stunned, Alicia nevertheless found herself taking the smith's advice, going to seat herself on the wooden bench that lay opposite to where the punishment was taking place. At first she tried to keep her eyes averted from what was taking place, but soon she found it was difficult to look away. The renewed swishing of the switch through the air was already telling her without a shadow of a doubt that the punisher was set on teaching a good lesson. When she dared to raise her eyes, she saw Master Reed had indeed returned upon what he'd been doing, with a grim, set look on his face. The woman was sobbing and wriggling as the switch fell mercilessly upon her, not failing to stripe her thighs and buttocks with red. She was now begging for her husband's forgiveness, but Master Reed was big, young and strong, and he held her in place with no difficulty. In spite of his chastised wife's wriggles and pleas, he continued to apply the switch diligently, apparently unmoved by her distress. It was only when he'd satisfied himself that his chastened wife was no longer writhing and struggling, but accepting her punishment with spent resignation, that he let her off his lap. The smith's wife, who, Alicia noted, was little older than Alicia herself, hopped from one foot to another, doing a strange sort of dance as she began to rub her bottom and thighs. Master Reed watched her with sombre satisfaction in his dark eyes.

"I trust this has taught you your lesson, wife," he told her sternly, still holding the switch. "You have her ladyship here to thank for the milder punishment you received."

Master Reed's wife turned her head to look to where Alicia was now sitting, her face crimson with embarrassment and her eyes brimming with tears. Alicia's heart ached in sympathy. Not long ago, she'd undergone similar humiliation herself. The smith's wife lowered her eyes, then turned to her husband.

"May I go now?" she asked in a subdued voice, her eyes still downcast.

Master Reed grunted his assent, and his wife scurried away to the house, one of her hands still clutching her bottom.

"Your ladyship, how may I be of assistance?" Master Reed said, rising and bowing his head respectfully.

He was a handsome man, Master Reed, with his dark hair and dark eyes, but, by the looks of it, quite stern to his wife. Alicia cleared her throat, struggling to concentrate on the errand that had brought her to the smith. She conferred with the blacksmith for a while, and was satisfied with his answers. He seemed able to do what she required, and readily agreed to send two apprentices to look at the house and take the required measurements, in order to provide right ironwork for the things that needed to be replaced. When Alicia inquired about the price, he scratched his head, however.

"Thing is, my lady," he said, with a rather sheepish smile. "'Tis this wife of mine who deals with things such as figures and numbers in our household. But, as you could see, she's rather out of sorts today, because of the lesson I had to teach her. However, she can come over tomorrow, before my apprentices, and you can bargain for a fair price. How about that?"

Alicia nodded, but could not help expressing her concern over what she'd witnessed.

"Will your wife be well enough tomorrow, Master Reed, you reckon?"

Master Reed looked at her in puzzlement.

"Why shouldn't she be?" he asked.

Alicia felt flustered.

"Well… you gave her quite a switching and she seemed… well… she seemed…"

Master Reed laughed, a mischievous sparkle dancing in his dark eyes.

"The switch stings something fierce, my lady, but, in truth, there's no lasting damage from it, and the pain fades quickly. Trust me, my lady, the damage is far more to my wife's pride than to her body. My woman shall be as right as rain tomorrow, and I daresay, sweet-tempered. Methinks you'll get a better bargain out of her, because she'll be less waspish than she usually is."

"If you say so," Alicia muttered, deciding to hope Master Reed had the right of it.

# CHAPTER 7

*L*ast night her husband had returned from Court quite late, after she'd fallen asleep, and Alicia had not had the chance to glance upon him. She did so in the morning, noting he liked to sleep naked, and he'd not woken her up to claim any kind of husbandly rights. He had behaved graciously by letting her have her sleep, and Alicia thought with a smile that she could, after all, behave graciously in her turn. She caressed the hardness of his smooth chest, and she saw him smile in his sleep, yet he did not wake up. She understood he must be tired from his prolonged duties last night, yet she knew she would have to wake him up because he should head to Court this morning. She decided to behave like a truly gracious wife and let him sleep for a while longer, as she took care of laying out and readying the garments he would wear today.

When she saw at last that her husband was still sleeping, giving no sign he would wake, she rejoined him on the bed, as a wicked thought came into her head. There were several ways of making a man alert and ready, weren't there? She pulled back the covers, and gently laid her lips upon his cock, which was lying at half-mast. And soon the scrumptious taste of his cock made her fully take him into her mouth. She smiled against his shaft when she felt him jolt wide awake, but continued her ministrations, until she made him spill his salty seed inside her mouth with a deep moan. She did not dislike the taste of it, and felt quite wicked as she swallowed his salty essence. She wiped her mouth, then looked upon him with a smile. She was still new to this kind of lovemaking, and she feared she'd been too artless.

"How do you feel, my lord?" she asked tentatively.

"I dreamt I'd died and gone to Heaven," he told her with that smile which made him look even comelier than he already was.

"Don't blaspheme," she chided with a smile of her own, further wiping her mouth with the back of her hand.

He caressed the seam of her lips, which were still red and slightly swollen from her earlier ministrations.

"You've behaved like a dutiful wife," he told her approvingly.

She laughed, still tasting his essence upon her tongue, and revelling in the salty taste of it.

"Dutiful wives get rewards," he told her, now stroking the side of her neck. "So, what does your heart desire, wife?"

She sighed, knowing it was already late, and also knowing he had his business at Court to attend to. Soon, she'd be similarly tethered to the court, since she knew Queen Eleanor expected her to come to attendance next week.

"The sun has long been up, and the bell has tolled eight. Do you have time to dispense rewards, husband?" she asked him pointedly, cocking en eyebrow.

He groaned, then chided her.

"You should have woken me sooner!"

She gestured to the garments that had already been laid out for him, readied.

"You have time enough for dressing and for breaking your fast."

Still, he chided her.

"You should have woken me sooner!" he muttered with a

frown. "If you'd woken me sooner, there'd have been time for more than dressing and breaking fast!"

At first she had indeed thought of waking him sooner, but he'd seemed to be sleeping so peacefully and she hadn't had the heart to do it. He didn't look like a fiend in his sleep, and, for that matter, nor did he look like an angel. He just looked, well, as her husband should, a comely man sleeping where he truly belonged – in her bed.

He sighed, straightening a tendril of her hair that had come loose, and gently brushing her cheek as he did so.

"No use crying over spilt milk now, I guess. There will be plenty of time for rewards when I get back," he said with that comely smile of his.

She frowned upon him, suddenly perceiving she'd miss him today. She hadn't thought she'd ever miss a man's presence. She'd always thought of men as rather useless. This one seemed to have his uses though. But she chastised herself for the silly way she'd already begun to moon over him. What had he said earlier?

"You said dutiful wives get rewards," she told him with a frown. "Does that mean undutiful wives get punishments?"

The next move he made stunned her. He swiftly sat up, taking hold of her and placing her over his lap, without giving her time to struggle or protest.

"Naughty wives certainly get punishments," he said cheerfully, laying a couple of spanks on her upturned rump.

Alicia braced herself for the searing caress of his hand upon her bottom, her heart thumping in strange anticipation. They were light, playful spanks though, just teasing, and holding only the faint promise of a fiery sting. He soon released her, and she saw he was grinning broadly. She keenly felt that stab of pleasure in her sheath, recalling the peculiar stirring she'd experienced right after he'd spanked her. Pleasure mingling with pain. Shameful, yet excruciatingly delicious.

*Naughty wives get punishments* – he'd said in jest. But what did *naughty* mean? And did she truly want to be naughty?

She watched him rise, with a look of deep regret on his face.

"Alas, I cannot linger and play, wife. The dreary Court awaits…"

She nodded, knowing they both had pressing chores today.

It was perhaps two hours later that Alicia received a visit from Master Reed's wife, to talk upon the price that the master smith required for his services. Alicia soon came to see, with a suppressed smile, that Mistress Reed was an astute woman and liked to drive a hard bargain. So they haggled over the price for a good while, taking each other's measure, until it was time for the two of them to burst out laughing. They'd reached a figure that was acceptable to both of them, but it had taken a long while for them to be able to do so.

"I must say, Mistress," Alicia said shaking her head with a smile. "Your husband erred when he told me you'd be easy to bargain with today. You haggle something fierce."

"Well, so do you for that matter, my lady," Mistress Reed retorted with a smile of her own.

Alicia had already come to like the master smith's wife, because she'd always been fond of plainspoken, decisive women. Yet she could not reconcile the image of this woman with that of the chastened, subdued wife who'd received a harsh punishment with a switch from her husband. Mistress Reed must have seen Alicia's curious glance, because she smiled self-consciously.

"I will be off now, my lady…" she said with a slight bow of her head.

Yet Alicia could no longer contain her curiosity. Besides, she had to make sure Mistress Reed was fine and did not have a husband who treated her ill.

"Your husband… Master Reed. He seems a harsh man," she said cautiously.

Mistress Reed burst out laughing with a shake of her head.

"Nay, milady. He is usually mild as a lamb, and a hard worker. He spends all his time at his forge and dreams only of smithing and clever contraptions all day long."

Alicia could not reconcile what Mistress Reed had spoken about with the image of the stern man whipping his wife's bare bottom with the switch.

"But…"

Mistress Reed sighed.

"You saw what you saw and, aye, he chastened me well yesterday, but it's upon a rare occasion that he does so, and, truth be told, I did everything in my power to drive him out of his mind…"

Alicia widened her eyes, and Mistress Reed went on with a broad grin.

"As I said, my husband is a hard worker. Sometimes he works too hard, as if work was his mistress… He sees to his craft, and I see to the running and the numbers of the business. But sometimes wicked thoughts come into my head and I think my man should pay more mind to love play with me than to his hard work. You see, this man of mine is not easily riled by my temper, which is something fierce. There's one thing he hates though – when I exchange playful words or hot glances with other men."

Alicia's eyes got even wider.

"So what you're saying is you like to make him jealous?! In order to get him to punish you?"

Mistress Reed nodded with a smile and a shrug.

"But why?" Alicia asked, although she recalled only too well the image of the punishment had stirred strange, shameful sensations inside her.

Mistress Reed coloured slightly, but then heaved a sigh and decided to speak.

"My lady, the switch he wields at times stings something fierce, and there is pain in the punishment, yet, for me, there is also strange pleasure. There is no lasting harm from my husband's chastisement, as he would rather cut off his right arm than hurt me in earnest. He would not ever say so, but I know he also enjoys the punishments I goad him to deliver at times, understanding within himself that I behave the way I do just to taunt him. You see, there is a closeness we both enjoy that this punishment brings. A strange bond which makes our love burn even fiercer. Besides, our loving between the sheets afterwards is simply wondrous... more wondrous than anything in this world."

Mistress Reed suddenly paused as if at last aware that she'd shared too much with a stranger, yet she cast Alicia a measuring glance. Then added with a wicked smile, "My lady, I see by the look in your eyes you know what I'm talking about. I saw your husband at times walking around the market. He is a handsome man, is he not? Has he already proven a stern husband?"

It was Alicia's turn to look flustered. She cleared her throat, not wanting to lie to a woman who'd already shared intimate things with her.

"He... well... he did chastise me soundly in front of the entire Court. The punishment..."

She was however unable to continue and glanced helplessly at Mistress Reed who gave her a mischievous wink.

"I understand you're newly married. So you'll both have time to sort out how the married discipline takes place..." Mistress Reed then added with a laugh, "Though I confess my bottom does smart something fierce this morning, after Tom took good care of it yesterday. He does not want to let it show, but he's already feeling somewhat guilty and fretting upon me today, to let me know how caring and sweet-tempered he can be."

Alicia laughed in her turn.

"Why, Master Reed swore to me the spanking would make *you* sweet-tempered."

Mistress Reed gave a mock frown.

"He wishes!" she proclaimed, and soon after that took her leave, promising she would visit again to oversee how things were going when her husband's apprentices came to take measurements for the ironwork that was needed.

Alicia told Mistress Reed she was looking forward to new visits from her, and hoped they would form a friendship. By the way Mistress Reed responded she was pleased that a noble lady was taking interest in her, but Alicia had never thought herself truly above hard-working people like Master and Mistress Reed. She'd always thought such people were often cleverer than her own peers.

The rest of her day kept her busy, yet she could not help but recall the strange, stirring conversation she'd had with Mistress Reed. She found herself blushing upon thinking of the way the blacksmith had wielded the switch upon his wife's bottom, and strived hard to put the image away from her mind. The image lingered with her though, and she found herself wondering what it would feel like to have a merciless switch striping her skin, while she was lying defenceless and her husband was brandishing it with vigour. She shook her head in wonder realizing she both dreaded the switch and felt strangely stirred by the prospect of it.

# CHAPTER 8

*B*ertran spent his day thinking only of the moment he would return to his wife and finish what they'd started this morning. He felt loath to dance attendance to Henry, who seemed to be keeping him at Court for naught. Bertran already felt weary of the court, and looked forward to the day when he and his wife would rejoin one of their estates, to spend their time away from the hustle and bustle of London.

Midday repast still found him thinking of his wife, and of her sweet lips upon his cock. She was no shy, blushing woman and she'd brought him great pleasure. He thought upon his match with satisfaction – at least in the bedchamber, things would be always to his liking. And, in truth, so far he'd nothing to reproach his wife for even outside the bedchamber. She'd not behaved like the proud, disdainful woman he'd thought she was. Besides, he'd expected her to hold a grudge for the humiliation he'd bestowed on her in front of the whole court, but she didn't seem angered against him anymore. He'd already perceived she was clever, so he assumed that, like him, she saw it was wiser to try to make the best of their marriage and attempt to be gracious to one another, since nothing could be changed. Or perhaps it was just as his parents had told him – the sound spanking he'd delivered had subdued her and had made her see him as the strong, decisive man he was.

His friends started teasing him good-naturedly, when they noted his absent-mindedness.

"No doubt thinking of the new bride he left at home…" Lord Vipont said cheerfully.

"Perhaps he's thinking of further chastisement to bestow upon the comely lady," Sir Simon added, with a wink.

His friends then made a show of proclaiming their wives had been on their best, sweetest behaviour since they'd witnessed Lady Alicia's punishment. They went on to commend Bertran for his disciplining skills.

"I daresay, unlike your late wife, who was tame and meek, this new lady of yours will give you plenty of occasion to display your skills and set her bottom ablaze," Sir Simon said.

Bertran said nothing, just smiling benevolently. His friends were mischievous, but for all their bragging and teasing, they were never harsh to their wives, and, to his knowledge, employed but mild discipline on their women.

"Wilful women are usually lusty in the bedchamber," Vipont quipped. "By the dreamy look on our friend's face this morn, the bride may be not as reluctant as we thought."

Both Simon and Vipont went on with their teasing, but Bertran remained silent, since he'd always been a private man and had always thought the things that took place in the bedchamber should stay in the bedchamber. He bore his friends' teasing with good humour, however noting the other lord knight who'd joined them, Tristram de Brunne, sat silent and rather forlorn, with brooding dark eyes. Bertran exchanged a look with his other friends, knowing that De Brunne was probably thinking of his own wife, the Northern lady he'd wed two years ago, who, it was well known, treated her husband with coldness and disdain. De Brunne and his wife were presently estranged from one another, and Bertran thought, so far, luck had smiled upon his own fate. Lady Alicia may not have wished him to marry her, but she seemed more than willing to spend time in his arms.

"Don't brood, Tristram," Simon said, touching his friend's shoulder.

"I'm not brooding," De Brunne muttered. "I'm thinking. I'm thinking I was wrong not to consider my lady wife may benefit from a lesson not very unlike the one Bertran's new wife has received of late."

Sir Simon and Lord Vipont heartily encouraged De Brunne that this was the right way of thinking, while Bertran rose with a smile, to go about his business. He meant to leave Court earlier today, to be able to come home earlier to his new wife, so he had no time to waste. Henry had bid him to go and deliver a message to the queen, as both monarchs now conversed mostly through their attendants, rather than talk face to face. Bertran suppressed a sigh, knowing the strife between the king and queen would lead to nothing good. Yet he was bound to obey his liege's request, and he went to the queen's quarters, to wait for Eleanor to deign to speak to him. He paused a little before he entered those quarters to straighten his cloak, which seemed to have come into disarray as he'd gone up the stairs. The door to the queen's quarters was slightly ajar and voices could be heard from behind it, the voices of Queen Eleanor's ladies.

"Poor Lady Alicia," one of the ladies was saying with feeling.

"Oh, poor Lady Alicia," another harrumphed. "Better say, poor Sir Bertran… Everyone knows she still carries a torch for De Jarnac's son."

Bertran stood still, with an icy feeling in his heart. The lady, whose voice he now recognised as Lady Edith's, went on with a sigh.

"I hope, for both their sakes that Lady Alicia will behave like a good and sensible woman, and put aside her foolish passion for Sir Erec. But who knows what she'll do. I'm told that one is a woman as devious as she is haughty. Perhaps she'll decide to keep De Jarnac as her lover. From what I could see when I entered their bedchamber, FitzRolf already seemed ensnared by her and she'll be able to twist him around her little finger."

At this moment, Queen Eleanor spoke sharply, urging the lady to keep her gossip to herself, and Bertran decided to make his presence known. Surely, Lady Edith was just a busybody, and one shouldn't set great store on her words. Yet, after he'd conferred with the queen, he couldn't shake a feeling of unease that stayed with him all day. There was a fire burning between Lady Alicia's legs. What if that fire burned harder for De Jarnac than for him? And what could he do if his wife still carried a torch for De Jarnac? Should he put a mighty fire on her bottom if he caught her as much as glancing at her former suitor? He reasoned he could punish his wife if she behaved unseemly and flaunted herself to De Jarnac, but he could do nothing if she only thought of the man. Unseemly thoughts were not the same as unseemly deeds, were they? What if De Jarnac would always have her heart, without even possessing her body? What then?

The evening found him cross and loath to rejoin his home, although all morning he'd been thinking only of coming home to his bride. He lingered in the yard of his house for a while, leaning against the trunk of an apple tree. Unwittingly, his eyes fell upon the branches and twigs of the tree, and he recalled well that an apple tree switch had been employed at times for his own discipline as a child. He reasoned he needed to let his new wife know he would not stand for her to take a lover. He would plainly let her know he intended to discipline her harshly if she meant to be disloyal to him. So he cut a good switch, meaning to show it to his wife and tell her it would be used for future chastisements if the need ever arose. He hoped the mere threat of it would dissuade her from thinking of the handsome Erec de Jarnac ever again.

When he entered their bedchamber, he found Alicia had been waiting for him and she cast him an eager smile. Her smile faded when she saw what he'd been carrying in his hand, and Bertran suddenly felt like a brute. Of course, it was his right to chastise his wife, and a time may come when he might have to do so, but, since they'd wed, Lady Alicia had done nothing to deserve a punishment. She had not strayed yet, and it was unfair to assume she ever would. He now felt stupid and awkward, standing there, switch in hand. He hastily placed the switch in a corner, by the door, for his wife to see he had no intention of using it.

His lady was now looking upon him with a stormy look in her green eyes, yet she spoke courteously.

"I've waited upon you, my lord. I'll call the serving girls to bring trays, as it is now too late for a repast in the solar."

He nodded, in some embarrassment. The next hour passed in near silence. Alicia sat by him, graciously, as he had his meal, and later, when it was time for his bath, she attended to him just as the lady of the house should. Yet she flinched from him when he attempted to touch her, and he did not press, seeing the anger in her gaze.

From time to time, her eyes kept darting to the switch that remained in its corner. Bertran knew once he'd placed it there, it should remain there, until it was time to use it. He would look like a fool if he simply tossed it away. He sighed, thinking perhaps he'd not been that wrong in his first thought. The threat of the switch would make his wife think twice about straying. He would not be a blind, complacent husband, as Lady Edith had implied – and he meant his new wife to see this from the very start of their marriage.

Silence still loomed between them as they both readied for bed.

"Do you mean to chastise me now?" Lady Alicia suddenly asked, looking at him levelly.

She was now dressed in her night shift and Bertran

suppressed his deep desire for her, knowing she was now very angry with him.

She cast a pointed look in the switch's direction. Bertran shook his head.

"No. Not now…" he said rather awkwardly.

It was hard to keep his arousal at bay, and he strived to focus on what she was saying.

"Not now? Later then? When?" she asked him, and her voice sounded calm.

"I do not know," he answered truthfully.

He did not know how to act around her. And she'd given him no true cause to punish her. Yet he was becoming so ensorcelled by her that he was beginning to fear what Lady Edith had said was true. She might be a cunning woman. Perhaps she did mean to deceive him. But would punishments be to any avail if she was indeed cunning and set on deceiving him? He glanced at her levelly. She did not strike him at all as a deceitful woman though, but as a truthful, plainspoken one.

He cleared his throat.

"Think upon it as a warning. Something that should prevent you from overstepping the boundaries. There'll be no need of it if you're a good wife and you stay within them."

"What are those boundaries?" she asked him levelly.

"You should be respectful, faithful and honourable," he told her just as levelly.

He could not quite forget she looked down upon his birth. So, perhaps he needed to emphasise he would have her respect.

She nodded, but there was ice in her voice as she spoke.

"As my husband, you should also be respectful, faithful and honourable in return," she told him.

He looked at her with a frown. There was no doubt he meant to be respectful and honourable, and he would never break faith with his lady. But it was not for his wife to demand it of him.

Wives were not supposed to make harsh demands, but ask graciously instead.

"I've already pledged myself to you. I do not mean to break my oath," he told her in vexation.

"So did I. And I do not mean to break my oath either," she countered, going to her trunk to fetch a comb. She sat herself in front of the mirror, unbraiding her long chestnut hair.

Bertran looked at her, mesmerized. Her hair was wondrous, and he longed to bury his hands in it.

He came to stand behind her, placing his hands on her shoulders, as she was brushing her hair in front of the mirror. She paid him no mind, as if he was not there. He frowned. It was not the welcome he'd expected from his eager new bride. Yet he had only himself to blame – he'd become angered by mere gossip.

"Where did you get the switch?" she asked him, deigning to speak to him at last.

"I've cut it from the apple tree in the yard," he answered truthfully.

"I see," she said levelly.

He could not resist, he took the comb away from her, and began brushing her long hair with long, slow movements.

"How many strokes?" he asked, having heard there were women who liked to give their hair one hundred strokes until they were satisfied it was untangled.

She frowned into the mirror.

"I thought you didn't mean to use the switch tonight!" she told him.

She'd mistaken his meaning, and Bertran opened his mouth to set her at ease, and mend this rift that had appeared between them because of the accursed switch. But the defiant glare on his wife's face made him think better on it. Was she disputing his right to discipline her? A mischievous thought came into his head.

"How many strokes will it take, do you reckon? How many

strokes will it take to cure you of your defiance?" he asked softly, as he continued to comb her hair with one hand. His other hand was already caressing the side of her neck.

ALICIA BREATHED deep before she answered. She was now torn between anger and lust. Why would her husband want to use a switch on her now? Did he mean to treat her as his chattel, as a woman to be punished whenever she decided to speak her mind? And did he mean to whip her for nothing, just to assert his power over her? That part of her was angry. The other part of her was recalling the switching she'd witnessed yesterday. What had Master Reed's wife said? That lovemaking was wondrous after a punishment... She recalled her wedding night and had to agree with Mistress Reed's judgement. She suppressed a sigh, because in truth she was now truly angry with her husband. It seemed he thought himself her master, and it was not a thought that pleased her. She'd rather talk on how things stood in their marriage concerning his right to discipline, not be simply confronted with his decision. She thought upon his question with a frown. He'd asked how many strokes she thought would cure her of her defiance.

"I do not know," she answered his question truthfully. "I reckon I shall find out anyway, isn't that so, lord husband?"

When he didn't answer, she went on:

"How will you do it then? Will you use the switch every time I say things you do not agree with? Every time I try to speak my mind?" she went on defiantly.

He'd already set his mind on spanking her, hadn't he? So she might as well speak defiantly to him, since she had nothing further to lose by it.

"Will you call witnesses to this punishment? Will you call others to witness my pain and humiliation?" she asked him bitterly, recalling how shamed she'd felt in front of the whole court on their wedding day.

He placed the comb on the table, and then turned her to face him.

"No, wife. Never. I shall not shame you again in front of others. There'll only be you and me if I punish you. And rest assured, I would never dream of chastising you for speaking your mind."

His words were levelheaded and his voice earnest. And she thought upon how his hard hand upon her bottom had made her feel. She'd been painfully humiliated to be spanked in front of everyone, yet if the punishment took place when there were only the two of them, then there'd no longer be any humiliation. There would be only the spanking... And the spanking... Her heart began to beat frantically. She was torn between anger and lust. And the feeling was strangely stirring.

"So, what are you waiting for, lord husband?" she asked, feeling brazen and defiant.

She boldly hoisted her nightgown, showing him her bare buttocks. She already knew they no longer bore the marks of his spanking. They were pristine, but in a short while they would no longer be so, would they?

"Aren't you going to fetch the switch?" she dared him.

Her husband muttered a short oath under his breath. He hoisted her on his shoulder, landing a stinging spank on her buttocks, which made her suppress a moan. He then carried her to the bed, seating himself on its edge, placing her face down across his knees.

Alicia braced herself for the spanking that was to follow, recalling only too well how strong and merciless his hand could be. But, instead of his hand on her bottom, she felt his finger slide gently inside her sex. She bit her lip to prevent herself from crying out in rapture.

"You're wet, my lady wife," he told her softly.

He spanked her with his free hand, while the finger of his other hand was still thrusting inside her. Alicia now moaned in earnest, while her sex filled with more delicious, honeyed liquid. There was just a faint sting in the spanks he was bestowing upon her and they felt more like a heated, brazen kiss than like a punishment. His hand upon her bottom was mischievous in its shameless caress, while the finger of his other hand was even more shameless. It slid in and out of her, in a rhythm that matched that of his spanking hand. When he paused, she gritted her teeth, knowing that soon she might utterly embarrass herself by climaxing in this undignified position. Why had he stopped spanking her?"

"This is no punishment for you, is it?" he asked, withdrawing his finger, which was now slick with moisture, and letting her off his lap.

Alicia stood up, in utter shame, with her cheeks flaming.

"I don't know," she muttered, not wanting to lie to him.

He said nothing, just perusing her with his gold-flecked eyes. Instead, he rose and cupped her face. He looked at her intently, then spoke against her lips, sending pleasurable tingles throughout her whole body.

"There is no punishment I have in store for you tonight. Only pleasure. And if it gives you pleasure to feel my hand spanking your bare bottom, then I shall strive to give you pleasure. But you need to ask for it."

He paused, then calmly sat himself on the bed.

"So ask for it, lady wife. Ask me to spank you."

She widened her eyes at him. She could not do it. A spanking was a punishment. What lady in her right mind asked to be chastised by her husband? Yet her sex was already painfully throbbing, and it seemed her bottom already ached for the punishing touch of his large hand.

"I... Husband, will you spank me?" she muttered, blushing even more fiercely than before.

The fiend grinned broadly.

"I couldn't quite hear you, wife. What was it that you just asked of me?"

Alicia glared at him.

"You know too well, you're not hard of hearing!" she countered in deep irritation.

He laughed.

"Defiant words from a wife to her lord," he said, still grinning. "Come here, over my lap, then. Methinks a few good spanks will cure you of your defiance."

Alicia found herself hesitating.

"Do you mean to spank me hard?" she asked, her heart beginning to thump in strange anticipation.

"Just come here, wife," he told her, and she found herself obeying.

He hoisted her nightgown, rubbing her bottom, which must still bear the faint imprint of his first spanks. He then delivered a light spank on the crown of her buttocks. He continued to spank her lightly, slowly spreading a pleasant warmth in her bottom, and molten delight throughout her whole body.

Alicia noted he was counting as he spanked, in a warm, husky voice.

"…five… six… seven…"

She nearly swooned with pleasure when he reached number eight. It was then that he spanked harder, landing two rapid, stinging spanks right on her sit spot. He then stopped abruptly.

Alicia keenly felt his engorged cock pressing against her body.

"Enough," he growled. "Just get on your hands and knees on the floor, like a good, dutiful wife should."

Alicia found herself instantly obeying him, setting herself on her elbows and knees, and thrusting her spanked bottom towards him. He knelt behind her, positioning her to his liking. She moaned deeply when he entered her from behind, filling her to the hilt. Her bottom smarted somewhat from the spanks he'd delivered, and she just loved the way his front was making contact with her tender buttocks. Soon, she lost all coherent thought, as he hammered in and out of her, fierce and deep.

As they both climbed into bed after the lovemaking was done, Alicia found her face flaming again. Her husband lay down, embracing her and settling her head on his chest.

"Are you in pain, wife?" he asked, and there seemed to be some concern in his voice.

"From the spanking? No, husband, you spanked me lightly," she told him in earnest.

"I wasn't talking of the spanking. I loved you to the hilt, and hard. Do you feel pain now?"

She shook her head.

"A bit sore maybe, but in no true pain."

He heaved a deep sigh.

"I'll be more careful in the future…You have a sweet cunt, my lady, it's easy to forget myself around you."

She blushed, torn between pleasure and embarrassment, and she recalled how wantonly she'd moaned when she'd been lying across his lap and he was warming her bottom. She felt ashamed of herself.

"Husband… do you think 'tis sinful?" she asked softly, her heart suddenly seized with anguish.

He held her tighter against him.

"Nay, I do not think lusty coupling is sinful."

Still, her heart kept beating in anguish.

"Not coupling… not that… The spanking… I…" she paused, in utter shame.

Was she a wicked, unnatural woman for enjoying him spanking her? In the Hall, when everyone had been watching, she'd been ashamed and frightened. She had not enjoyed the punishment in itself, yet she had enjoyed the feeling of his hand spanking her. It was strange. And tonight, she'd been able to enjoy herself fully. There'd been no humiliation about the way he'd spanked her bare bottom. Only a delicious naughtiness. And only the two of them. A bond that seemed to have forged between two lovers, the one Mistress Reed had spoken about.

"I enjoyed it as well," Bertran told her. "My hand chastising your luscious bottom. So I guess we're both sinners, if this is a sin," he added calmly.

"You seem unconcerned by it! But what if what we did is wrong?" she asked in anguish. "You were married before! Is this usual love play between spouses?"

He answered after a long pause.

"I've never spanked a woman before you, my lady. I had no cause to."

She'd heard of his first wife. Everyone had called her a paragon of virtue. Alicia suddenly felt jealous, although she knew it was petty of her to think so of a woman who was no longer among the living.

"She must have been a good woman," she muttered, in utter shame.

"She was," he replied.

The anguish didn't leave her.

"Do you think me wicked? Wicked for enjoying this?" she asked in earnest.

He sat up, making her sit up with him.

"Peace, wife," he said gently. "I do not think you are wicked. My first wife was a good woman, but that doesn't make my second bad. You're different from her, is all."

He buried a hand in her hair, bestowing upon her his comely smile.

"You like heated caresses, as do I. And I suppose that's why you like me spanking you. There's great heat in it and closeness between us that this brings. I see no shame or sin in it, and I doubt God Himself would call that sinful. God is wise."

He kissed her gently, then lowered her on the bed, covering her with his strong body.

"My confessor is surely going to give me hard penance for my wanton behaviour. I think I'll have to spend most of my days on my knees in prayer," Alicia muttered between kisses.

He laughed.

"*Amee*, tell him you've been a dutiful wife and your husband's strong hand will always make sure you remain so. He'll be satisfied."

She rolled her eyes at his carelessness for her immortal soul, but was soon lost in his kisses. She hazily realized he'd called her *amee* – his beloved. It was just an endearment, but it made her heart beat faster to think upon the word. He loved her very gently, moving in slow circles inside her and making her melt at the sweetness of it all. It was strange, wasn't it? He could be both hard and gentle. Alicia sighed contentedly after they'd both found their release, and she closed her eyes, telling herself he may not be wrong. There was a rightness between them when they coupled which couldn't persuade her that what they did was sinful. They were a good match. She frowned a little, recalling the switch only too well, and his warning he would use it if necessary. From his words, she'd understood he hadn't chastised his first wife thus. Alicia knew too well the punishment he would deliver if she crossed him would not be love play, like the one he'd bestowed on her today. She had no doubt he would make sure it would be a harsh punishment and not pleasure. She fell asleep, vexed with herself. She didn't feel angry with him anymore – not even at the prospect of a hard, merciless punishment. It was strange. It felt like she trusted he would never truly harm her.

# CHAPTER 9

*B*ertran woke up to find his lady wife still sleeping in his arms. He smiled in relief, recalling that today he would not have to go to Court. It was time to join his men on the practice field, since his courtly business had lately taken him away from such duties. He got ready, having a care not to wake his sleeping wife, and covering her naked body with the blanket.

He looked upon his lady, feeling both lust and tenderness. Her long hair had become tangled in her sleep, as he'd not given her the opportunity to braid it last night. He had no doubt she would spend quite a while combing it and setting it to rights, and he savoured that lovely image in his mind. He told himself he had been wrong in his jealousy. No woman who was pining for another lover would respond to his lovemaking as she did.

As he prepared to go out, his eyes fell unwittingly on the switch he'd placed by the door, and he grinned. He would have occasion to use it, but not for punishment. He already understood chastising his lady over his knee brought her more pleasure than pain. It would be useless to try to use such discipline when she misbehaved, so he would have to think of other ways of keeping her within boundaries. But perhaps this would not prove a great hardship and no such boundaries would ever be needed. So far, Lady Alicia seemed a levelheaded woman.

He felt light-hearted today, and thought again of his fears last night as unfounded. Lady Alicia burned for his touch. She'd met him thrust for thrust while he'd had her from behind. And she'd glanced passionately into his eyes when he'd been inside her later, loving her gently. No shadow of Sir Erec de Jarnac had loomed between them. So his fears were unfounded. The match seemed as pleasing to her as it was to him.

After he hurriedly broke his fast, he joined his men on the practice field, feeling the liberation of strong exertion. But, as he parried and attacked, he couldn't help but notice the hustle and bustle in the courtyard. People he did not know seemed to be coming about, with their tools. Soon he came to see that some of them were carpenter's apprentices. He frowned. To his knowledge, he'd hired no carpenters to do work on his house. The mystery was soon unveiled when he conferred with the people in question, who cheerfully informed him that it was his lady wife who'd hired them. The lady Alicia had also employed a smith's services, he found out from his servants, as well as made several purchases, to replace some of the linens and furnishings. He listened to all this with widening eyes. The lady had been his wife but for a few days, and she was already behaving as if she'd been mistress of it forever. And, he noted with a frown, she'd not even spoken to him of the changes she envisaged making. He went back to his practice, venting his newly acquired frustration on his practice opponents, who had to defend themselves fiercely against him.

He met his wife once the midday repast was ready, and looked upon her in displeasure. No, she was nothing like his first wife, who would have asked him for permission for every small change to his household. Besides, his former wife would never have been able to oversee such swift, decisive changes. She'd been frail, and had shouldered the responsibility of his household with difficulty. Lady Alicia didn't seem plagued by such frailty. He spotted her busying herself about, commanding his servants with effortless ease. She seemed in high spirits, and cast him a wide smile when she saw he'd come into the Hall.

As the meal was served, and she sat herself beside him, he couldn't help but notice the improvements. The food was fresher and hotter, and the servants less slack in their duties. The rotten rushes in the Hall had been already changed, and the table gleamed with the polishing it had received. The house seemed to be coming to life, and, while he was displeased his lady hadn't spoken to him about any of her actions, he couldn't help but like what he saw around him.

His people, he also noted, seemed more cheerful than he'd seen them in years, no doubt pleased with the better food and already cleaner surroundings.

"I hope the food is to your liking, my lord," his wife said solicitously. "It is not seasoned nearly as well as I like it, as the spices in the chest need to be renewed, but I've made sure it's properly cooked."

He nodded, rather ungraciously. She'd already hired several new servants, as he could perceive, not seeming to care for the added expense. He ate in silence, debating whether he should be pleased with his wife for seeing to their comfort or displeased with her for incurring such expense without consulting him.

"You've wrought a lot of changes," he found himself saying. "Carpentry, iron work and sundry other things…"

She cut what he'd meant to say, with an easy smile.

"Aye, I'm doing what needs to be done."

He frowned at her, perceiving she seemed unconcerned by his unease.

"You didn't see fit to ask for my permission," he said pointedly.

She looked at him in wonder.

"What for? I'm sure you already knew what was necessary. The house was in a sorry state and couldn't be left as such. This duty belongs to the lady of the house, not to the lord."

He said nothing, still frowning.

"Are you displeased?" she asked in a puzzled voice. "I didn't think you'd be. It's menial housewifery. I did not think you'd take offence."

She seemed sincere in her puzzlement, and Bertran began to see she had not meant to defy him. But that made things even worse. She'd not even thought to ask for his permission.

"What of funds?" he asked, recalling she had not asked him for coin for these changes.

She waved her hand.

"I used the funds I carried with me, but rest assured everything will be accounted for. I'm thrifty, and I'm not one to incur unnecessary expenses. I can bring you the ledgers to look at, if you want. I've written everything down properly, since we've no steward here to take care of it."

"I assume you can write, cipher and read," he muttered.

She nodded.

"Certainly. Can't you?"

He could, though he didn't take much pleasure in it and relied on clerks to do what was necessary. His former wife had been unable to write and read, as many women of her station were. On the contrary, Lady Alicia was a woman who could do so. He recalled she'd shouldered the burden of vast estates for years, so this had been a necessary skill.

"I'll look at the ledgers, wife," he said, knowing he should be pleased with her skills. "I am not sure such expenses were necessary at such a time. I'm not as wealthy as your father is."

"But now your marriage to me has brought you great wealth. We can afford the expense, since my dowry is ample enough," she countered in a level voice.

He looked at her in annoyance. She'd just reminded him she was above him in wealth.

"You now have funds to set this house to rights," she went on in the same level voice. "So this is what I'm doing. Setting it to rights."

She touched his arm with a smile, then rose, when a serving girl required her assistance. He followed her with widened eyes. When she regained her seat, she smiled again, as if unconcerned by the talk that had taken place. It was the first time he saw her eating with relish, and he recalled her lack of appetite the day of their wedding, when she'd been forced to sit on her freshly spanked, blazing bottom. Now she seemed a different woman altogether. Cheerful and content. And, by the looks of it, quite bold and unconcerned with his own wishes.

"I am displeased you didn't see fit to let me know of your decision," he said, trying to tell himself he should be cross with his lady for not consulting him about any of the changes.

"Oh, why is that?" Lady Alicia asked, casting him a benevolent look.

He opened his mouth to speak, but nothing came to mind.

"You shouldn't be displeased," Lady Alicia told him cheerfully. "I am doing what a dutiful wife should. And you need not worry. I am a prudent woman and responsible. For years I've taken care of vast lands and overseen our vassals and our people. This is, in fact, a menial task, easy to accomplish. In truth, too menial to concern the lord of the house with, don't you think?"

He heaved a deep sigh, understanding she'd outwitted him. He couldn't find fault with what she'd done, since she was doing it for a good cause.

"Have better care in future to keep me appraised of what's going on, my lady," he found himself muttering, still somewhat vexed by her behaviour, but unable to reproach her for anything.

She beamed at him.

"Certainly, my lord. I shall never fail to do so in future," she said graciously.

With this, their talk was ended, and Bertran found himself further sighing within himself. This woman was nothing like his first wife. She was decisive and bold. But, he saw, she was also quite clever, and had managed to smooth-talk him, without making it appear she was disparaging him.

"It's market day," Lady Alicia spoke. "I thought I'd take a reprieve from my chores and go to the market. The spices in the chest need replacing, so I will take the chance and get some fresh air."

Bertran keenly noted she was merely telling him of her plans, instead of asking for his permission. He opened his mouth to point this out to her, but saw the smile on her face. She was so comely, with those sparkling green eyes and those lush, full lips he'd never have enough kissing.

"I shall accompany you then," he found himself saying, in spite of what he'd meant to utter first. "My other chores will wait, since I'm also in need of a breath of fresh air."

She seemed pleased he'd offered to accompany her, and Bertran found himself forgetting his earlier vexation. He just looked forward to a walk in his wife's company.

THE DAY WAS sunny and mild as they walked to the market, choosing to do so unaccompanied by any of their people. It was not far, so it was not worth going on horseback. As she looked upon her husband while they walked, Alicia noted he smiled easily, and did not look dour and grim as on that first day she'd glanced upon him. He seemed to be enjoying the outing as much as she did. She talked more than he, noting he was not a man given to prattle, yet the time spent together passed companionably. There was heat clinging between them, as always, but somehow Alicia found herself thinking less of the caresses they'd shared in the bedchamber and genuinely enjoying his mere company. He was courteous to her, but not overly polite, cheerful without being overly talkative. And she also recalled this morning when she'd watched him from a window, amazed by the liquid, fluid grace he'd displayed with his sword. She'd heard tell of his exploits in the battles with the Welsh, but she'd not had occasion to see him with a sword in hand. The sword became him, as if he'd been born carrying one. Alicia understood he was a fierce fighter in battle. But, come to think of it, so had been Erec de Jarnac, whom people unjustly called "a fop" because of the excessive elegance of his clothes. Erec was also courteous, and he smiled as easily as this man. Only, Alicia knew too well, she'd never felt so warm under Erec's smile. Her husband's smile held a light in it that seemed to make the day even brighter than it already was. She soon found herself easily talking to him of her home, and of the pursuits she'd enjoyed. She was a keen rider and huntress, and had little patience for embroidery and those tamer, more gentle pursuits, she told him with a rueful smile.

"King Henry is as keen a hunter as you are," Bertran said. "You'll soon have occasion to join in one of his hunts."

"I'm looking forward to it," Alicia said. "I'm rather handy with the bow. I suppose this skill makes up somewhat for my lack in other areas. I have a poor ear for music, and my needle skills are not as good as those of other ladies. The tapestry I've started on is only slowly progressing. I fear it will take years to finish – and the outcome may not be so pretty to look at."

He laughed.

"I don't care much for tapestries, and I suppose we can rely on the help of my sisters for such adornments, if you wish. My sisters love embroidering. As for music, I enjoy it as much as the next man, yet I must confess I was born tone deaf and can't carry a tune."

She laughed in turn, grateful of the ease with which he'd become reconciled with her faults. He also enjoyed hunting, and they began a lengthy talk of hawks and hounds. Time flew by as they walked, and Alicia found herself forgetting she'd ever contemplated a different husband. This man seemed suitable to her, and not only in the bedchamber. Yet, she found herself remembering their circumstances, when he brought up Sir Erec.

"So… De Jarnac's son, how long have you two been acquainted?" he asked rather abruptly.

"Since childhood, but we did not see each other often," she said, with an uneasy shrug. She no longer wanted to think of Erec, because it reminded her of the humiliation she'd received at her husband's hands in the Hall. Alicia did not think herself vain, but she was proud, and she still chafed to recall he'd spanked her in front of others. Still, she also recalled what Bertran's mother had said – Bertran had not wanted to inflict this humiliation upon her.

"The insults…" she said in wonder. "You've never once reproached me for the insults written in that letter you received."

He waved his hand.

"You did receive punishment for those insults, didn't you? I think it's only fair to put such things behind us and start afresh."

She nodded, understanding he was indeed an honourable lord. She opened her mouth to speak of him and tell him the truth of what had happened, yet thought better on it. He'd said he'd given a fresh start to their marriage. It would seem petty of her to try to bring up her innocence at such a time. Besides, they did not know each other well and he might think she was just bringing excuses. So she held her mouth shut, contenting herself to smile at him.

"You did not rant and rave after I punished you in front of all to see," he said abruptly, giving her a measuring glance. "And you no longer seem to hold that against me."

She shrugged, keeping her smile.

"I came to understand you were doing the king's bidding," she told him truthfully. "Your mother came to talk to me. She told me the punishment was not your wish."

He gave a short laugh, and then muttered, "Trust my lady mother to interfere." However he soon added, with a sigh, "No, it was not my wish. I am a private man and do not relish making a spectacle of myself in front of others. But the king had commanded so…"

She perused him, heaving a bitter sigh of her own.

"You realise both you and I were but pawns in the battle between Henry and Eleanor?" she said.

He frowned. "How so?" he asked in a guarded voice.

"The punishment you bestowed on me in front of the whole court. Henry did not genuinely care you'd been insulted. What he cared for was to humiliate my father, and, thus, to also humiliate the queen, who owns my father's loyalty. The queen did not come to my defence because she knew it was just what Henry wanted. There is a feud between the king and the queen, and we were both caught in its snare."

He shook his head.

"They might be feuding, but I do not think it will come to war. Both Henry and Eleanor know the costs of war. They are both wise, and will not start one to fulfil their ambition."

Alicia gave a mirthless laugh.

"You think highly of our monarchs."

He glanced at her in surprise.

"Don't you?"

"Yes," Alicia nodded. "They are both great rulers, but I fear their ambition still has the better of them. Didn't the king already have Thomas Becket murdered out of ambition? Mark my words, soon there'll be war between Henry and Eleanor, and we'll all pay the price."

~

His wife spoke boldly and assuredly. The women of his acquaintance were not so bold when they talked of politics, except, of course, for the queen herself. But Bertran did not find himself disliking his wife's talk. It was levelheaded and astute. A part of him also feared the king and the queen might come to war, but the other part of him chose to hope for the best. He hoped the two great rulers would reconcile.

"Where would you stand if there's a war?" his wife asked him bluntly.

He frowned.

"With my liege, the king. Where else should I stand?" he replied, cocking an eyebrow.

"The queen also holds you in high esteem, I'm told," his wife said, but then added with a smile. "Still, I did not think you'd stand with her. Because that would mean forsaking the pledge you made to your king, and you do not seem to be one of those men who break pledges."

He cast her a sharp look.

"And where will you stand if there's a war, my lady?" he asked softly.

He recalled only too well that the De Lancres supported the queen, even if Alicia's father had not openly declared his loyalties. Would his wife choose to stand against her own husband if a war broke between Henry and Eleanor?

"I've pledged myself to you, my lord, haven't I?" his wife answered in a level voice. "There's no return from it, is there? I also never break my pledges. So I shall stand where you stand, and protect our family's interests."

She gazed straight into his eyes as she said so, and a pleasant warmth enveloped Bertran's heart. Her green eyes seemed true. And she was telling him she would behave honourably, and stand by his side. It seemed he had been wrong in his assumption she might ever prove disloyal. She seemed to hold honour as dear as he did.

He bowed his head in courteous acknowledgement.

"My lady, I shall strive to prove myself worthy of your loyalty," he said formally.

CHAPTER 10

They'd reached the market and Alicia found herself drawn to the joyous hustle and bustle. There were merchants raucously praising their wares. Fine cloths and linens and silk. Food and sweetmeats of various kinds. Ribbons and trinkets of many sorts. Colours and sounds and smells that she found herself enjoying in a rare day of leisure. It was the first day of true leisure she'd had in months and she found herself savouring it, just as she savoured the company of the man walking next to her. A man she found to be gracious.

"We can linger and look, if you like," he told her with good cheer, when he perceived her avid gaze upon the colourful silks a merchant was praising at his stall.

She shook her head with a smile.

"Nay. We've come to buy spices, not silk, my lord, remember?" she told him.

She assumed, like all men, her husband would be impatient to go on the particular errand they'd come for. So she wanted to be gracious in her turn, and not impose upon his patience.

But the merchant had already seen that a lord and lady had

96

paused by his stall, and seized his chance to praise his merchandise.

"Fine silk, my lady," he said hastily, letting a bolt of sky-blue silk unfurl in front of Alicia. "All the way from Byzantium. Just feel how delicate and soft it is!"

Alicia opened her mouth to voice a firm refusal, but Sir Bertran beat her to it.

"Go on, my lady," he said with a smile. "There's nothing rushing us greatly today. No tedious court business for either me or you. Only duties that can wait for a while."

Alicia frowned.

"Sundry household chores. That have been too long post-poned and can't wait that long," she told him pointedly, but it was his turn to shake his head.

"Perchance we both need a small respite from our duties," he said mildly and approached the stall to feel the silk the merchant was eagerly holding out to them.

Alicia's mouth was dry as she watched her husband's long fingers bestow a feather-like caress on the silk. She found herself suddenly envying that silk.

"Soft and delicate indeed," Sir Bertran said. "But perhaps my lady wife is a better judge of it," he added turning to Alicia.

She approached to feel the silk, attempting to trace with her fingers the same trail her husband had made. Even the thought of having touched the same fabric as him made her heart race.

"Yes, soft and delicate," she conceded. "But, we're in no need of silk," she told the merchant in firm tones.

"Linen perhaps? Fine linen! The finest!" the merchant said eagerly.

But Alicia shook her head, and began to walk away, making Sir Bertran follow.

"I told you I am frugal," she told her husband. "And it's only spices we've come for."

"But there's no harm in looking about," he told her cheerfully, taking her arm and leading her to a stall where a boy was selling gingerbread pastries.

After he paid the required copper coins, he extended one of the sweetmeats to her, while he bit into the other with zest. She made a show of sighing and of appearing reluctant to join the fun he was obviously having, but she took a bite of her own gingerbread. It tasted delicious and sweet, just as sweet as this day was proving to be.

She let herself be persuaded to walk around and look at the stalls by her husband's side, immersing herself into the colours and scents and in the sheer pleasure of his company.

"So this is what you do when you aren't at Court... Stroll and idle about?" she asked him with laughter in her voice.

He shook his head.

"No. I've little time for strolls or idleness. Perhaps that's why I'm as eager as a child to take full advantage of this walk."

She nodded.

"There always seems to be so little time to enjoy the simple pleasures of life. There are always ledgers, vassals and simple folk to guide, and lands to oversee, as well as the chores of keeping the household in order," she said, recalling all the pressing duties, which had always kept her busy.

"How old were you when you first began to oversee your household and estates?" he asked as they were walking to the spice merchant's stall.

Alicia mused.

"Fourteen. When my mother passed away."

"And you've no brothers and sisters who could have aided you? What of your father?"

She shrugged, unwilling to reveal how pained she still was by her father's cowardice and by how he'd callously let her take the blame for his own deeds. She was loath to tell her husband that, over the years, her father had relied mainly on her to oversee their estates. It had felt good to be in charge and to have a lenient parent, yet looking back on it, Alicia began to see it had been advantageous for her father to let her shoulder most of the responsibility. It had been convenient for him to let everyone believe his haughty daughter ruled him, because if things went wrong he would let the blame fall entirely on her. She chastised herself for being too blind to see this, and she resolved to put her father away from her mind. She was done with him.

"My father had his own tasks to see to," she said tersely, then decided to steer the talk to other things. "Let us look at what the spice merchant has to offer," she added, as they got close to the spice stall.

The stall's owner, an elderly man with a silver beard, welcomed them with a broad grin, knowing by their attire that these customers would be able to pay good coin for his wares.

"Pepper for my lady? Cinnamon? Ginger?" he said with a knowing smile, beckoning Alicia to smell and taste and touch what he held on display.

She nodded, but did not try to appear too eager. She expected the merchant to ask for an outrageous price for his goods. Some spices were as dear as gold, and she also wanted to buy a bit of saffron because she'd always enjoyed it in her dishes. Saffron was a new spice she'd learned of lately and it was indeed a luxury.

The merchant beamed at her when she asked for the price of it, and bid her to be careful when she touched and tasted it, because saffron stains were hard to remove from both the skin and the clothes.

"Saffron for my lady and my lord," he said with a slight wink. "It certainly heats the blood. And it will be so good for my lord, if he will add it to a hot drink…"

Alicia chuckled, because she'd never been one of those ladies bothered by ribald talk.

"My lord has no need of such, I'll have you know," she answered the merchant with good humour.

Bertran glanced at both her and the merchant with a puzzled frown.

"It is said that saffron is good for lovers. And it is also said that men employ it sometimes to increase their prowess between the sheets," she enlightened him with a smile, because she'd never shied away from plain talk.

Her husband cocked an eyebrow, perusing her with his fine hazel eyes. She ignored him, because she wanted to focus on her transaction, knowing the merchant would lead her a merry dance until they both came to agree upon a fair price for the lot of spices she intended to purchase.

"Sugar also, perhaps, my lady?" the merchant asked, when she'd settled on the small amount of saffron she would need.

Sugar was also dear, but it was a medicine that was necessary in a good household. Alicia knew it was needed for stomach ailments. It warmed the belly and the gut, and relieved the pain. She tasted the grains the merchant offered her, and as she did so, sweetness invaded her mouth and she unwittingly glanced at her husband. It was wicked to look upon him when her body was savouring this sweet pleasure, and to think she could not be touched by him with so many people around. She suddenly fantasized of the moment when they were alone and he would get to touch her.

"Sweet," she muttered casting him a playful smile.

His hazel eyes seemed to perceive the teasing in her voice. He accepted the merchant's bid to have a taste of the sugar medicine himself. But he shrugged after he'd tasted the grains of sugar, with a smile of his own, which to Alicia looked suddenly mischievous.

"It's fine. But I like hot better than sweet," he said.

*So*, did her lord husband prefer a naughty, defiant wife to a sweet, biddable woman? Alicia strived hard not to blush, replaying in her mind their heated couplings. Aye – they had been mostly hot rather than sweet.

The merchant cleared his throat.

"My lord, my lady, perchance there is something you may find of interest in my humble trade. It is a spice few know and use here. I got it from a Portuguese merchant. It is called *grains of Paradise*."

Alicia turned, her interest piqued. She'd heard of the spice, but had never purchased it. The name was full of promise.

The merchant showed them a deep bowl filled with brownish grains, larger than pepper. Alicia thrust her hand inside the bowl of grains, because she'd always enjoyed the feel of new things upon her skin. In surprise she soon felt her husband's hand touch hers as they both let their fingers run through the bowl of spice. It felt intriguing to Alicia to touch something new while her lover was touching her. She felt a hot current run through her body, and knew with certainty they would couple as soon as they got to their home.

"It's far better than pepper," the merchant explained. "Gently crushed or even whole, it can be used in spice rubs and in braises, and in a spiced cake it is simply delicious, mixed with cinnamon and cloves. But not only that – crushed into a fine powder, it can be used to help open wounds close, and to reduce boils and swellings."

Alicia struggled to come back to her transaction. She did not place such great faith in the merchant, and resolved to ask an apothecary about the true properties of this new spice. Yet it seemed there should be no harm in buying some *grains of Paradise* to try.

"Paradise," her husband mused. "Why is it called *grains of Paradise*? On account of its heavenly taste?"

The merchant smiled knowingly.

"My lord, some count it even better than saffron for those who want to make their loving hot. Use half a spoon of powdered grains in a jug of hot milk with cinnamon and you will get to judge for yourselves, both you and your lady. Both men and women are the better for tasting it."

Bertran laughed with good humour.

"What say you, wife?" he said, and winked mischievously at Alicia.

Alicia tasted some of the spice that the merchant had crushed for her. It burned hot on her tongue. Hotter than pepper.

"Perchance a couple of ounces," she muttered, striving hard to keep her head clear until they reached their home.

The haggling soon followed, because the merchant seemed set on requiring an outrageous price of them, but Alicia held her own. It was Bertran who put an end to her bargaining, when it had been going on for perhaps more than a quarter of an hour.

"Enough. We'll take the lot now," he called to the merchant, tossing to him the coins for the last price the merchant had been stubbornly calling for, after Alicia had made him considerably reduce the first figure he'd mentioned.

The merchant beamed, and added a small additional pouch of powdered *grains of Paradise* to the bag of spices he handed them, proclaiming the lord and lady should try its benefits as soon as can be when they reached their home.

Alicia glared at her husband, when he began to lead her away.

"You should have left me more time to bargain with him. He was sure to give us an even lower price."

"My lady wife, I am sorry for spoiling your enjoyment of haggling," Bertran told her with a chuckle.

"I don't enjoy…" Alicia started, but he cut her off.

"Aye, you do. And under different circumstances, I would have let you have your fun. Yet there is pressing business I have on my mind, and the hour was growing late…"

Alicia stifled a sigh, understanding he was right after all. She had been a fool to think of coupling in the middle of the day, when there were so many of their chores left unattended.

She tried to hide her disappointment, and concentrated on

feeling pleased with her new purchases which would help her replenish their spice chest.

THE WALK to their home felt to Bertran perhaps the longest of his life. It was with relief that he stepped inside his house, behind his lady wife.

"Let us head upstairs," he whispered softly in her ear, and had the pleasure of seeing her widen her eyes.

"What, now, my lord?" she stammered.

"Aye, now," he told her tersely, giving her a gentle push to the stairs that led to their bedchamber.

"But your pressing business?" his wife muttered.

"This is it," he replied casting her a wide grin, and feeling his blood pump even hotter in his veins when he saw colour rise in her cheeks.

Yet she instantly heeded his command, as a sweet, obedient wife should. He grinned as he followed her up the stairs, letting his eyes roam on the inviting swish of her hips. She was not, in fact, a sweet, obedient wife, but a spirited woman who craved hot loving as much as he did. And he'd not missed her open invitation at the market. He'd been in agony over getting home to honour this invitation as soon as could be. He'd have paid the merchant whatever he'd asked only to head home to see to his spirited wife. Yet he'd also enjoyed seeing his lady bargain, and he'd savoured the way her passionate eyes sparkled and her voice got heated as she was doing so. There was a hot fierceness about his wife, and he was beginning to understand he would never wish to trade that fierceness for anything in the world.

He tossed the bag of spices in a corner of their chamber after he closed the door behind them, but as he did so, a wicked thought came into his head. She had taunted him at the spice stall, hadn't she, this naughty wife of his. This wife of his who was naughty rather than sweet.

"Methinks we should try the power of this new spice," he said softly, as he went to search for the pouch of powdered *grains of Paradise*.

He soon found it, and had the pleasure to see a look of puzzlement on his naughty wife's face.

"What, now? Perchance it's best to talk to an apothecary before we add it to food or drink."

He chuckled, pleased he'd confounded her.

"Who said anything about a drink?" he tossed at her.

He'd never done this, but he'd heard one of the lords at Court talk of it. Certain salves or pepper worked well for the particular purpose the lord had told them about. Yet this lord's particular purpose had been punishment. Bertran's particular purpose was pleasure. Of the hot kind.

"It was, I thought, rather naughty and unbecoming of you to talk about your lord's prowess in bed to a stranger. Don't you find?" he said, making his voice a mixture of harshness and invitation.

Alicia's sparkling eyes widened even more.

"Was it?" she asked, and she looked puzzled.

Bertran cast her a wicked smile, as he applied some of the powdered grains of Paradise on his hand. It felt hot, and soon he knew his hand would begin to sting faintly – a sting that on his wife's skin would feel somewhere between pain and pleasure. So it was perfect for what he had in mind.

"What are you doing?" Alicia asked in sheer shock and surprise.

"Making sure the lesson I deliver will lead to an appropriate sting," Bertran said, as he went to seat himself on the bed and patted his lap.

He loved the way his wife looked at him, with both longing and apprehension.

"Husband…" she muttered uncertainly.

"Come here, lady wife. Right now," he called to her, making his voice both playful and stern. His heart began to race in his chest when she complied, and soon he had her draped across his lap with her skirts hoisted. He wasted no time sliding his heated palm over the skin of her lush behind.

"Ahh…"

Her voice was full of heat as, he was certain, she was already beginning to feel the hot pepper of his caressing touch. He soon started to spank lightly, and had occasion to hear his lady begin to moan. He was able to feel the peppery sting in his own hand, and he knew a scorching heat was beginning to build on the skin of his lady's naughty bottom. He didn't even have to spank hard for her to be able to feel the agonizing pleasure of the sting.

"So, lady wife," he asked wickedly, "does that feel like paradise to you?"

She did not answer, and he landed a hard spank on her already pink buttocks in order to make her come to attention.

"Both hell and paradise," she muttered at last, and it was plain she was striving to find her words.

Bertran heaved a deep sigh and let her slide off his lap, because at this time, his cock was too stiff and ready, and he could no longer prolong this hot torture. Soon, he had Alicia astride him, and he drove into her deeply, loving the feel of her already hot behind against his thighs as he was driving in and out of her. The lovemaking proved quite invigorating, and they were both ready to return to their pressing chores when they were done at last, although, by the half-glaring half-dreamy look on his lady wife's face, and by the way she rubbed her bottom before she straightened her skirts, the hot pepper in the grains of Paradise had made a lasting impression upon her.

"A worthy idea for a punishment when you truly misbehave," Bertran tossed at her, as he was setting his own clothing to rights.

She cast him a true glare this time, and he grinned broadly, loving to tease her even further.

"What?" he added innocently, as he was heading to the door. "Already loath to enjoy the benefits of this new spice you've purchased?"

He did not let her give her own retort, and left the room, closing the door behind him, smug with his teasing. However, he'd left the room in haste because he'd already begun thinking of new, hot lovemaking he could bestow upon his lady right now. And it was true there were several duties waiting for both of them today, so their loving would have to wait until night fell.

# CHAPTER 11

*A*few days later, Alicia received a summons from the queen to come to Court. She complied with a heavy heart and a deep sigh because, in truth, these days of mere housewifery had been a good respite from her usual life, which was much busier and included other, more pressing duties. She prepared for the tedious, humiliating chores as a lady-in-attendance at Court, as well as for the scorn of all those who'd seen her bare bottom thoroughly chastised on her wedding day.

The ladies-in-waiting tittered when Alicia came to see the queen in her chambers, and the lady Edith, whom Alicia remembered well from her wedding night, bore a downright malicious sneer upon her face.

"Leave us," the queen said tersely, shooing away her attendants and beckoning Alicia to seat herself in a chair in front of her.

Alicia complied, schooling her expression to look serene and betray nothing of the scorching humiliation she was feeling at the ladies' disdainful treatment.

Eleanor frowned at her.

"It could not be helped, you know. Your punishment. My

husband saw the letter as an open threat to his own authority. He's become restless these days… thinking his eldest son and I wish to challenge him in his rule."

Alicia nodded, knowing it was wise to stay silent. Young Henry, Queen Eleanor's eldest son by their king, who was now seventeen had been already crowned as the second king of their land, according to the Capetian custom. Yet Alicia knew too well King Henry had now started to resent both his wife and his son for this. He saw them as threats to his own rule, and now he sought to restrain the queen's influence, thinking she was already plotting with their son to overthrow him. Alicia believed it was the king's own tyrannical behaviour that was strengthening Eleanor's opposition to him, yet Eleanor was herself arrogant and vain. Both monarchs shared this unfortunate trait, and since for some years now Henry had tossed the older Eleanor from his bed to openly carouse with his mistresses, Eleanor felt even more entitled to show him she would not be so lightly dismissed.

"My husband will have my son be king of nothing. King in name only. He fears I seek to gain even more power through my offspring…" Queen Eleanor went on, echoing Alicia's own thoughts.

The queen cast Alicia a level glance.

"I do not wish strife or war though. I only wish my husband to acknowledge my son's position, and not treat him with disdain. Disdain…" she repeated the word, bitterly. "Enough of this," Eleanor added, with a wave of her hand. "I've come to England to see my son formally wed at Winchester, to Marguerite of France, and to make sure he is given the authority due to him."

Eleanor had never been a woman to mince words, a trait which Alicia admired in her. Yet she feared Eleanor's bluntness was making her royal husband perceive her even more as a threat. Again, the queen spoke as if she'd guessed Alicia's thoughts.

"Women need to show cunning rather than forthrightness at times. Our husbands think themselves entitled to show they are mightier than us…What of your husband?"

Alicia knew the queen valued plain talk and honesty, so she spoke in earnest.

"He is a worthy man. Not vain. He's levelheaded. And he is not the sort who feels the need to belittle a woman in order to show his might."

The queen gave her an appraising glance.

"You're pleased with the match," she said with a half-smile that was both surprised and wistful.

"Aye, my queen," Alicia answered simply.

"In truth he is a worthy man, your husband," the queen said begrudgingly. "And you were wrong to spurn him on account of his being a bastard. Had you sought my council, I would have advised you to pen out a gracious refusal."

Alicia did not want to betray her father, because she knew the queen's wrath was just as scorching as that of her royal husband. Eleanor would not be pleased to learn Alicia's father had hidden his intervention from her. Since she did not want to lie to her queen, Alicia just bowed her head.

Eleanor heaved a deep sigh.

"What's done is done, although a match to De Jarnac's son would have been preferable and strengthened our ranks. And I see you are, after all, pleased in your new husband. So we could turn an advantage into a disadvantage."

Alicia raised her head, and she knew there was no turning from this. She'd made a pledge to her husband, one she could not betray.

"I mean to stand with my husband from now on, my queen. And as you know, my husband is loyal to King Henry."

Her heart started thumping heavily in her chest. She knew

the queen would prove a formidable enemy. So she fully expected Eleanor's wrath. Instead, she heard the queen laugh and saw her shake her head.

"I never expected a man like Bertran FitzRolf to switch allegiance. And I know you. You are a woman who places above all else the welfare of those she cherishes. It is plain you already care for your new husband. It is touching. Once I believed in love, the same way you do, until my heart was trampled upon."

There was something heart-breaking in the queen's words, which made Alicia's own soul stir in sympathy. *Trouveres* and troubadours alike still sang of the great love between Henry and Eleanor, yet Henry had betrayed that love.

"But I need not dwell upon past misfortunes, but try to right present times," Eleanor concluded. "My son is getting restless, knowing his father wishes to deny him all access to power. A gesture is needed to reassure him of his father's love and respect. I wish my son to be crowned again, in Winchester this time, for all England to rejoice in the crowning and witness my son's glory. But I dare not suggest this to my husband, lest he think I mean to use this for my own gain. Yet Bertran FitzRolf has my husband's ear."

Alicia nodded, beginning to understand Eleanor indeed sought to turn a match she'd first perceived as disadvantageous into an advantage. Eleanor was wise, and it seemed all she wanted was her son to feel secure in his authority. If Young Henry felt secure, a conflict could be avoided and war between two feuding monarchs could be prevented. Alicia remembered Bertran wanted peace just as much as she did.

"The suggestion has to come from FitzRolf, because he's the one man whose loyalty my husband will never doubt," the queen went on. "It's for the common good. As long as Henry gives my son his due respect, he has my loyalty. Tell your husband this. I do not mean you to prevail upon him with cunning. Just tell him of our talk."

"I could never do otherwise than be forthright with my lord," Alicia spoke, with a gaze that gave the queen to understand she would never deceive her husband, no matter what her sovereign's plans might be.

The look Eleanor cast her was one of begrudging respect.

"Off you go then. I am told FitzRolf is not with Henry at the moment. Go find him as soon as can be. I cannot summon him myself without Henry becoming angry and suspicious. So it is best you do this task for me."

Alicia inclined her head and curtsied. Then she left the chambers to do what her sovereign had asked of her. As she hurried to descend the stairs, heading to the place where she knew her husband carried on his duties, she nearly bumped into two bodies, close to one another. It was an isolated spot, where guards or courtiers would not come upon the two lovers, Alicia began to think, attempting to avert her eyes from the hot embrace in front of her. Yet she found herself unable to look away, because she instantly saw it was not a woman who the man in front of her was hotly embracing, but another man. She stared, dumbfounded. One of the men locked in the passionate embrace was Erec de Jarnac, whom she should have wed. The other was Godfrey Haughton, a young courtier who was her own age and whom she knew but little. The two men sprang apart, looking upon her with eyes full of apprehension. De Jarnac was the first to regain his composure.

"Godfrey…" he muttered. "Go now. I shall talk to the lady."

Haughton nodded, then scurried away, up the stairs in the direction Alicia had come from. So she was left alone to face Erec de Jarnac. She stared at him, still shaken by what her eyes had perceived. Sir Erec gave a slight shrug and a faint smile.

"I trust you won't tell anyone what you've seen, my lady. We both know it will lead to my downfall."

She nodded. It was not for her to judge, was it? Some might call Sir Erec's behaviour sinful, but Alicia recalled only too well her own behaviour in the bedchamber would be frowned upon. If Sir Erec was a sinner, then so was she.

"I shall not reveal your secret," she said softly, glancing warily around.

It was not prudent to linger alone with Sir Erec. People might come upon them, and they were prone to gossip. Alicia was a married woman now.

"Thank you, my lady," Sir Erec said courteously.

Alicia wanted to go, but he stopped her with a gesture.

"I did not mean to deceive you, my lady," he went on. "I would have made a good husband to you and been able to sire children. We would have agreed upon a convenient arrangement, which would have made us both happy. I meant to tell you the truth about my preferences, but we were never alone together, and there was no opportunity to do so."

Alicia recalled too well that all their encounters had been brief, and there had never been a chance to confer alone with Erec. Both their fathers had always been there. She glanced at him, measuring him from top to toe. The ladies found him more handsome than Sir Bertran, but she did not. His features may be more harmonious, and his green eyes alluring, but his frame was lither than Sir Bertran's. He was graceful where Sir Bertran was strong. And there was no heat or passion that she'd ever felt when she glanced upon Sir Erec.

"I wish you well, Sir Erec," she said in earnest. "And I do not think you meant to deceive me."

She liked Erec de Jarnac, and had thought this would be enough to make him a good husband. Erec had always seemed amiable and tolerant, so she'd thought his mild disposition would suit her own temper, which was haughtier and fiercer. Still, while there was liking between her and Sir Erec, there'd never been any heat. And perhaps it was because Sir Erec seemed to prefer men to women. But, Alicia understood, it was not only because of that. She simply preferred Bertran. He was the only man she'd ever looked upon who made her blood hot.

"What of your present match?" Sir Erec went on in the same soft voice. "Are you well, my lady?" he asked, and there was genuine concern in his voice.

She nodded, with a small smile.

"I'm well, Sir Erec. It might not be the match I wished, but he…" she trailed off, blushing slightly.

She didn't truly know what to tell Sir Erec. There was great heat between her and Sir Bertran, and, in the last days, she'd discovered there was more. There was mischievousness, and there was laughter, and there was simply contentment and joy whenever they just talked or walked together. She could not imagine herself ever married to Sir Erec now that she had her new husband.

"I see…" Sir Erec said casting her an appraising glance.

He then added with a smile.

"Perhaps it's best we did not wed."

She nodded, and then glanced sharply behind her, as it seemed to her there was a rustle she could hear. She saw no one, but she knew the castle was a busy place. Soon they were bound to be discovered.

"Be careful at Court, my lady," Sir Erec whispered, as if in echo of her thoughts. "The court is like a nest of asps, and even more so today, as Henry and Eleanor are readying for war against each other."

"You stand for Eleanor?" Alicia asked.

It was his turn to nod.

"I stand with my family," he said with a rueful smile. "And my family stands with Eleanor…"

He added, giving her a pensive look.

"Your husband's family stands with Henry," he said. "So I'll assume you'll now stand with Henry."

She acquiesced, as he gave a sigh, which he accompanied with a sad smile.

"We're all forced to play our monarchs' game, aren't we?" he said, echoing her own thoughts.

They soon parted ways, knowing it was imprudent to linger when someone might come upon them. Alicia hurried down the stairs to give the message she'd been entrusted with, her heart now pounding at the prospect of seeing Bertran. They saw each other so little while they were both at Court.

She came upon her husband in the Hall, while he was conferring with other lords. He frowned upon her when he perceived her, and he drew her aside.

"You look flushed," he told her, and there seemed to be disapproval in his voice.

"I hurried here. There is a message from the queen," she told him, then proceeded to relate Eleanor's words to him.

Bertran listened closely to what she said, not interrupting her. He heaved a small sigh when she finished.

"What the Queen asks is level-headed. And Young Henry is already formally a king. A coronation in Winchester may appease his bruised pride," he said at last, in a soft voice. "Yet I do not know if King Henry will relent."

"But will you speak to your liege?" Alicia pressed.

Bertran nodded.

"I will. Because I wish for reconciliation between the King and the Queen, not for more strife between them."

She nodded in return. It was slim hope, but it was hope, nevertheless. Perhaps the two parties would finally decide to settle their differences. She longed for peace, rather than war, because she knew if war broke out, her husband would have to join that war. She glanced upon him, resisting the urge to straighten an unruly lock of brown hair that had fallen on his forehead. She checked herself, perceiving many eyes in the Hall were upon them.

"So," she said rather awkwardly. "I must go back to my own duties."

He frowned upon her, and it seemed to her there was disapproval in his eyes as he did so.

"You came from the Queen's quarters, and not half an hour past I saw Erec de Jarnac head in the same direction you came from," he said, and the frown didn't leave his face.

She stared at him, and found she'd nearly forgotten her encounter with Erec, although it had been memorable.

"Yes, I did come upon him," she said, not wanting to lie to her husband.

"You did?" Bertran asked softly.

"Yes, we exchanged a few words in greeting and then we both went on our own ways," Alicia said levelly.

She would, of course, protect Sir Erec's secret, but there was nothing in her own behaviour she sought to hide. She was an honourable woman, and she felt sure her husband would be able to perceive she was so.

He seemed to ponder on what she'd said, then glanced upon her with gold-flecked hazel eyes that looked warmer.

"I see," he said, lightly touching her hand.

Alicia nearly moaned at the touch, in recall of the heated caresses they'd exchanged the last time he'd been inside her, loving her more urgently this morning when they'd woken.

"Not so many hours till dusk…" she muttered, speaking to herself.

He stared at her, then, at last, his lips curved into a lazy smile.

"So, my lady, thinking of dusk already?" he said softly.

It was her turn to smile, letting her teeth dig a little into her bottom lip and stepping away from him.

"Already…" she said, trailing her words, then adding in a teasing voice. "But I must be away, my lord. We both have other, pressing business to attend to."

She briefly curtsied, as he bowed. She savoured the hungry

look of longing he was now casting in her direction. Suppressing a sigh, she retraced her steps to rejoin the queen's quarters, already thinking of the moment when she and Bertran would be alone at last.

❧

BERTRAN STARED AFTER HIS WIFE, noting the lovely swish of her rounded hips as she was walking away from him. He thought of her lush bottom, and of that delicious pink colour it had been a few days ago when it had been freshly spanked.

The image lingered with him, and he found himself rather distracted, and striving hard to focus on the pressing task from the Queen and on the duties he had to attend to. He found himself wishing for dusk to come sooner, and felt incensed when the evening meal found both him and his wife still at Court, doing their sovereigns' bidding. Henry insisted Bertran take a seat at the high table so, during the meal, Bertran was unable to sit by his wife, who arrived in the Hall later, and had to take a seat at one of the other tables, together with some of the other courtiers. He also noted in displeasure that Erec de Jarnac had chosen a seat not far away from her, at the same table, so it was easy for them to confer if they chose to. His earlier anguish over De Jarnac returned, although, when he'd talked to his wife, he'd been persuaded that she'd spoken the truth to him about her encounter with her former suitor.

From where he was, he looked upon his wife and De Jarnac, who exchanged words from time to time. He could not see Alicia's face, as her back was turned to him, and she was facing de Jarnac, but Sir Erec's face was plain to see. He was smiling at her as he talked, and Bertran found himself hating him fiercely.

"So, my lord, how's newly married life?" a voice nearby cut into his thoughts.

Bertran frowned, only now perceiving the lady Edith was

seated right next to him. He did not like it, already knowing this lady was the worst gossip at Court. He answered her attempts at conversation stiltedly, striving to focus on the food and knowing now he would not have occasion to look upon what his wife and De Jarnac were doing. Lady Edith missed nothing and he didn't want to give her more fuel for gossip.

He turned a deaf ear to most of what Lady Edith was saying, but his ears sharpened when she at last spoke of something he disliked.

"I hope our Lady Alicia has resigned herself to her match to you, my lord. She needs a firm man, after all, who will take her in hand and punish her soundly for her transgressions. I'm sure in no time she will see our king's wisdom. The knight she clearly preferred, Sir Erec, is no match to you in strength and bravery. He's just a fop."

Bertran suppressed a foul curse. He did not like to be recalled that his wife had preferred Sir Erec's suit over his. He didn't have the chance to answer though. Queen Eleanor had obviously heard the lady Edith, and she spoke loudly for everyone at the table to hear.

"Sir Erec is no fop, my lady Edith. He is a valiant knight who can hold his own against men like Sir Bertran in any tournament."

Bertran did not miss the edge in the queen's voice. Erec's father was loyal to her cause. The king might have humiliated both De Jarnac and the queen, when he'd decreed Alicia should marry a De Morne, but the queen would plainly not stand for further humiliation.

Henry, in his turn, did not miss the edge in his wife's voice. He spoke now, with an equal edge in his own voice.

"What say you, wife? I cannot believe my ears. Sir Bertran is worth ten times the likes of Erec de Jarnac in any tournament."

The queen snorted derisively.

"Well, we'll never get the chance to see it, will we? You despise tournaments and you never want to hold any."

There was a tense silence at the table, followed by a long squabble in which the queen's sons also joined, since both Young Henry and his brother Richard, the second son born to King Henry and Eleanor, loved tournaments above everything in this world. Bertran stared in wonder, when, at last wearied down by his family's protests, the king proclaimed in a grim voice, "Fine, have it as you wish. We'll have a tournament in a week hence. And then we'll all have occasion to see whose champions are better. Won't we, Sir Bertran?"

"Yes, my liege," Sir Bertran replied dutifully.

He thought of the upcoming tournament with a kind of angry satisfaction. He welcomed the chance to wipe the smirk off De Jarnac's handsome face. His wife would finally get to see how wrong she'd been to choose Sir Erec over him.

It was late when both his wife and he rejoined their home and, by the dark circles he could now perceive under Alicia's eyes, Bertran understood she was weary. So, in spite of his ardent wish to plunge his cock inside her, and perhaps indulge more in the kind of mischievous discipline they both enjoyed, he pleaded tiredness, in order to let her get her own rest. She protested, but not too much, as she dropped with fatigue as soon as they both climbed into bed. He held her tight against him as she slept, telling himself she was entirely his now. She didn't sleep in Sir Erec's arms every night, did she? It was in her husband's arms she slept.

# CHAPTER 12

*I*t seemed her husband was at last able to get King Henry to agree to having his eldest son crowned in Winchester for a second time, and Alicia breathed a sigh of relief, knowing the queen was pleased with Henry's acquiescence. The days that followed passed uneventfully, yet Alicia felt weary of the court, and of Lady Edith's constant sneers and snide remarks. It was, as one of the ladies-in-attendance who came to befriend Alicia told her, that Lady Edith had a daughter and she'd hoped to make a match with Lord FitzRolf, which gave good cause for her aversion to Alicia. It was also that Lady Edith must have already perceived Queen Eleanor held Alicia in high esteem, which increased her jealousy. It did not help that Eleanor dismissed her ladies from time to time to confer with Alicia.

On one such occasion, the queen chose to speak to Alicia about the events, which would take place on the morrow.

"This tournament. It is a good thing," Queen Eleanor mused. "Did you see my son Henry's face light with pleasure upon it? Unlike his father, my son loves jousting and he is almost certain to win the tournament."

Alicia nodded, knowing it was so. At seventeen, Young Henry had already showed his prowess in tournaments, and was certain to win even more glory as he advanced in age.

"I wonder who would win the joust I wagered upon with my husband. Do you think it will be Sir Erec or your own husband in tomorrow's joust?"

Alicia shrugged, feeling worry rise in her chest. Both her husband and Sir Erec were worthy knights, and, even if he was lither of form, Sir Erec was a redoubtable *tourneyer*. In truth, she did not know which of the two knights would best the other, and she had begun to worry her husband's pride and standing would take a great blow if the outcome was not the one he desired. The king was urging him to win and he would be angered if Bertran did not prove himself the victor. Besides, she'd come to see how her husband clenched his fists whenever Sir Erec's name was mentioned. She avoided speaking that name in his presence, because she saw he had become jealous of her former suitor. She wished she were able to tell him he had even less cause for his jealousy than he thought, yet Sir Erec had sworn her to secrecy and she'd never betrayed her word.

"I do not know, my queen. I hope it will be my husband," Alicia muttered with a sigh.

Eleanor sighed in return.

"It would give me great satisfaction if it were Sir Erec, just to see the smirk wiped off my royal husband's arrogant face. Yet perchance you are right. It is better your husband should win. Henry will be appeased. And he won't begrudge my son's own glory in the rest of the tournament."

Alicia nodded, understanding that, once again, Eleanor was proving herself a wise politician. She saw now that Eleanor had deftly manoeuvred Henry into giving a tournament to make her son shine in front of all to see, and the wager concerning her own husband and Sir Erec had been just a clever ploy. Henry despised tournaments, and the fact he'd been forced to give one must still chafe. So she prayed her husband would win the joust with Sir Erec that would take place on the very morrow. She sensed that much depended on it.

That night at home, she had occasion to see her husband was tenser than usual. He was not sharp with her, because it was not his manner to behave so, yet she saw the taut line of his mouth and the set look in his eyes. He seemed far away, and Alicia guessed he was probably dwelling upon tomorrow's events. She pretended not to notice his mood, and let him have his peace, because she sensed it was peace and a distance from her that he needed at this time.

So she did not look at him with invitation in her eyes, nor attempt to touch him teasingly or press herself against him when they were finally alone, as had become her habit in the last days. Nor did she engage him in talk as she usually did. She kept her distance instead, just busying herself with righting things about their chamber and with ordering their garments in one of the chests.

She was mightily surprised when she at last sensed her husband's hand upon her shoulder from behind. She'd thought him still occupied with his goblet of wine and his own thoughts. She turned to face him, and found him grim and frowning upon her.

"You've not even glanced upon me this night, my lady," he muttered, and his voice sounded displeased.

"I thought to leave you your peace. The tournament's tomorrow," Alicia answered him an earnest.

It was the first time in their marriage that he was speaking so grimly to her. He was usually of good humour whenever he addressed her. But she understood he was entitled to feel grim tonight. He did not have an easy task ahead of him tomorrow.

"You have been cold to me," he said and his voice sounded sharp. "Perchance you're pining for another?"

The name of Erec de Jarnac remained unspoken between

them. Alicia nearly opened her mouth to tell Bertran that Erec had in mind a vastly different kind of lover and not her, yet it did not feel fair to impart this secret to him, especially since Bertran would fight this man tomorrow. It was not her place to interfere in the fight in any way. Besides, it would be wrong to break a word she'd given.

She touched her husband's long lashes in a caress meant to brush off the jealousy that was smouldering there.

"Peace, husband, I burn only for you!" she whispered, letting him hear the truth in her voice.

He glanced at her searchingly, as if to make sure she spoke true. But then, all of a sudden, he closed the lid of the chest that she'd been setting to rights, and he hoisted her on it, impatiently moving her skirts aside and making quick work of parting her thighs.

Soon he was pulling his own garments aside, letting her see his engorged cock. "Why, here?" she asked in sheer surprise, understanding he meant to plunge into her swiftly.

Yet she already felt wet and ready just by glancing upon his rigid manhood, and she heard his quick grunt of satisfaction as he brought his hand between her legs and could feel she was already gushing for his thrust. And thrust into her he did, with a vengeance that nearly took her breath away and made her swoon with pleasure. He loved her very deep, and punishingly, and Alicia understood she would feel sore after this kind of loving, yet she revelled in every moment of it, and in the way he possessively whispered as he was thrusting in and out of her.

"Mine. You are mine, my lady. Fully mine!"

"Aye!"

She cried her full acquiescence, as rapture made her sex convulsively clench around the hard shaft that was going in and out of her at a punishing rate. She'd nearly swooned with pleasure, crying out her joy, yet when she came back to herself, she perceived her husband was not done loving her hard. So he went on, loving her just as hard, until tears simply came to her eyes, and something she'd not thought possible happened at last. She felt rapture seize her again, even more powerful than the first time, and she shouted her joy a second time, just as he was spending his hot seed inside her.

It was with difficulty that she came back to herself, and scrambled to her feet to go and clean off his seed from between her legs. Her legs trembled and her knees nearly buckled as she did so, and she softly cursed under her breath. She heard him chuckle behind her, and she could hear male arrogance in his voice as he said:

"Methinks I loved you rather well…"

She heaved a sigh, unable even to speak at this time, and thinking he would be the death of her if more tournaments like this one took place and he was tense with battle longing. Yet he held her tenderly when she joined him in their bed, and his voice was full of warmth when he told her, "In truth, I'm glad you're fully mine, my lady. I do not think I could ever wish for a better wife."

She pressed herself against him, savouring his warmth. She opened her mouth to speak words in return, telling him she'd never want a better husband. Yet it was different words that came upon her lips instead. *I love you, husband.* She was astounded the very moment she opened her mouth to speak them, and at the last moment bit them back. She'd never thought marriage was for love. Love was a courtly tale, that only troubadours believed in, wasn't it? Marriage meant caring and loyalty and sometimes lust. But love? At that moment she understood in puzzlement that, in truth, she felt now certain she loved her husband, and had just failed to acknowledge it to herself in the past days. Aye, there was caring and loyalty and lust between them. Yet there was also love. She loved Bertran already and could not picture in her head a world where he was not her husband. She opened her mouth to tell him the words, thinking he would be glad to hear them, yet stopped herself in time. He had a tournament tomorrow. Now was not the time to utter stirring words like these. Perhaps he did not want to acknowledge such feelings at this time. His thoughts should perhaps be on what needed to be done on the morrow. On knightly battle rather than on courtly love.

"I am well pleased with you too, husband," she said instead, kissing him lightly on the cheek and snuggling against him.

ertran felt well rested and light of heart the next day, telling himself that, whatever the outcome of the joust, he felt now sure his fears regarding Sir Erec and his lady had been silly. His lady's eyes had shone fierce and true when she'd told him she belonged to him only, and a husband could not truly ask for more.

His joust with Sir Erec was to open the tournament, which would span three days, with more jousts during the first day, and with sword fights on the second. The main event, the melee, would take place on the third day. Henry would allow for only a small tournament, prepared in haste, with a small number of knights, but it was better than nothing, since Henry himself usually disapproved of tournaments.

Bertran kissed his lady ardently before he urged her to join the stalls that had been readied for the audience, looking upon the tournament field. Lady Alicia graciously offered to help while his squires assisted him with the pieces of his armour, but he declined her offer with a smile.

"My squires are well able to handle things. So off you go, my lady," he told her. "'Tis best you get a good seat to watch this joust. I mean to win it, you know."

Alicia had never seen him joust or engage in a sword fight, and he meant to show her he was a husband worthy of her, even if she'd not thought him good enough at first. She'd come to see his worth in the bedchamber and by her side, yet, he thought with a suppressed grin, she'd never had occasion to see his worth as a knight. Today he meant to show her he was indeed worthy of her hand.

Alicia glanced upon him, returning his smile.

"Well then, my lord, I hope your lance will strike well and true and you'll be the victor," she said brushing a feather-light kiss on his lips.

He stared after her as she went away, telling himself there was no other course for him but to win the joust with De Jarnac. Now that he knew he had his lady's full regard, he felt confident he would win.

There was plenty of time left before the joust, and Bertran went to check on his destrier one last time. He had faith in his squires, but he always liked to see to his horse himself before a fight or a tournament. Once he'd made sure the spirited animal that he called Noir was well rested and shod, and fully ready for the charge, he headed towards the tent to get into his hauberk and into the rest of his armour.

"Good luck, sir knight!" He heard a voice from behind him, and at first he attempted to pretend he had not heard the call.

It was a voice he'd recognized as belonging to the lady Edith, and Lady Edith was the last person he wished to talk to before the joust. Her malicious gossip had done him harm enough as it was, and he didn't want to exchange any words with her. Yet he was forced to stop and bow his head graciously when the lady caught up with him.

"I will be cheering for your victory against the fop, De Jarnac," Lady Edith said with a sickeningly sweet smile.

He nodded and started to walk away.

"I saw your wife just exchange words with him and it seemed she was wishing him luck," Lady Edith added behind him.

Bertran shook his head, telling himself it was best not to listen to whatever she was saying. He walked ahead, but it seemed Lady Edith's loud voice was intent on following him.

"Of course, it's gracious of her to look upon her husband's opponent, and I am sure it was kindly meant. After all, she and Erec grew up together and they've been close since childhood."

Bertran took a deep breath recalling only too well that Alicia had told him she was not so well acquainted with Erec, even if she'd known him a long time. Lady Edith was obviously lying.

"And I am sure your lady wife is well pleased with you as her husband now," Lady Edith's hateful voice still followed. "I told her she was sobbing for naught when I helped prepare her for the bedding on her wedding night. It was plain she was still pining for Sir Erec, and some of us heard her whisper his name between sobs."

Another lie, Bertran told himself firmly, as he walked away with long hurried strides to reach his tent, not sparing Lady Edith another glance. Before the bedding, it had been natural for Alicia to feel distressed, because their rushed wedding had taken place right after a harsh spanking from him. Yet he doubted she'd ever called De Jarnac's name.

He dismissed the hateful words, knowing Lady Edith to be malicious and full of sheer spite for others. He put them away from his mind as he readied for the joust, and strove to focus on vanquishing his opponent. He thought on Sir Erec and of this knight's fame as a *tourneyer*. It was not the first time he met Sir Erec in the field. They'd jousted against one another three other times, and had fought with swords twice in a tournament. Bertran was proud to have won both sword fights against De Jarnac. Yet, he'd only won one joust. Sir Erec had managed to win the other two.

As he headed for the field, now fully armoured, Bertran thought more on Sir Erec. He had to admit that De Jarnac was a worthy opponent. Sir Erec's family was also of better rank and wealth than his own family, and Erec had not been born a bastard. Bertran knew only too well all ladies admired Sir Erec's appearance. *Some of us heard her whisper his name between sobs.* The hateful words rang in his mind, and no matter how much he pushed them away, they would not let him be. It seemed as if he was walking in his sleep when he got on his destrier and his squire handed him his lance for the first charge out of three against Sir Erec. Sir Erec... whom his lady had sought to marry. He strived to focus on the charge as he spurred his horse, trying to make his lance strike true and his shield hold firm, knowing the knight who was riding menacingly in his direction was a force to be reckoned with.

The charge passed in a lightning-fast whirl. Stunned, Bertran belatedly understood he was already lying on the ground, and De Jarnac's lance had already managed to unhorse him. He cursed, foully, tasting blood and realizing he'd bitten hard upon his tongue during the fall. Yet he soon rose, aided by his squire's helping hands, feeling his flank and back throb fiercely.

"This is just one, my lord. There's two more to go," one of his squires told him encouragingly, and he nodded, knowing now he had to win points in both the next charge and the one after the next.

He did not dare to look towards the stalls where the courtiers were avidly watching and cheering. He knew his lady wife had seen him fall, unhorsed by the man she'd meant to marry and whom she'd thought worthier than him. Lady Edith's hateful words rang in his ears. He imagined the triumphant smirk De Jarnac was now wearing upon his face as he was waiting for the next charge. A dark, determined rage descended over him. He would make him fall. Both times he would make De Jarnac fall. And he grimly hoped one of the falls may end up killing him.

ALICIA STRIVED hard to keep her composure, as deep relief coursed through her, when she saw her husband had risen from his fall, and was heading for the next lance charge. The moment he'd fallen, she'd feared he was grievously injured. Even death by a fall was not uncommon in jousts. Oh, why hadn't she tried to dissuade Bertran from entering the tournament? She now found she did not care at all for his knightly pride, for Henry's command or for Eleanor's plans. She just wanted her husband to be safe.

Two more charges. And she watched with a thumping heart as both opponents galloped towards one another. She prayed within herself that Bertran would finish the joust hale and safe. She no longer cared for the outcome of it. She only wanted Bertran to be safe. She shouted with sheer joy when her husband's lance struck the other knight with swift precision. The lance broke on his opponent's chest, which meant Bertran was already the victor of this charge and he would get points. For a moment, it seemed De Jarnac would remain on his horse, yet in the end he was unable to hang on, because Bertran's lance had shattered against his chest with rending force. And Sir Erec went down.

Alicia suppressed a deep sigh, happy that, for now, Bertran was whole. However, she also felt relieved when Sir Erec was able to rise from his dangerous fall. The points were, at this moment, even. This meant the fate of the joust would be decided on the last charge. Alicia would have wanted to close her eyes until the whole thing was over, yet she could not do so when her husband's safety was at stake. So she watched on, striving to appear calm and confident, knowing if Bertran happened to glance at her from where he was, he would feel encouraged by her good cheer. The last charge soon began, and Alicia clenched her fists, wishing with all her might no harm should come to the man she loved.

Her heart skipped with joy as her husband's lance struck a blow even mightier than the one before, swiftly unhorsing his opponent, then she felt ashamed at rejoicing so when a man as amiable as Sir Erec lay on the ground and might be wounded. Yet she could not help but feel happy for her husband's victory. It was then she unwittingly perceived Godfrey Haughton, whom she'd seen locked in an embrace with Erec, go as white as a sheet and look about to faint when Sir Erec wouldn't rise from his fall and had to be carried away from the field by his squires. She also perceived some eyes were already glancing in curiosity towards Haughton, whose own family supported King Henry and who was supposed to rejoice in Bertran's victory.

She instantly understood questions might be asked if more eyes fell upon Godfrey Haughton and his obvious distress. So she took it upon herself to cry the motto her husband had claimed for himself, ever since he'd decided he would keep the name FitzRolf rather than revert to De Morne:

"*Non sans droict!*" she cried in a loud, triumphant voice, drawing all gazes upon herself.

*Non sans droict.* Not without right. She saw her husband raise his helmeted head from the field to look upon her, but she could not help but cast an anguished glance in Haughton's direction. She did not want her husband's victory to cause the downfall of two men. And she fervently hoped Haughton had recovered enough to prevent more prying eyes upon his distress.

"Young Haughton seems to take Sir Erec's defeat so very hard. I wonder why." She heard Lady Edith's hateful, venomous voice behind her.

She made up her mind quickly, knowing there was a way to help. She fervently hoped Sir Erec was not grievously wounded, and he would immediately send word to his lover he was hale. Yet she had no way of knowing. So she decided to slip away, unobtrusively, to look upon her husband's vanquished opponent. Since everyone had already gathered around the victor, it was easy to do so, and she made her way, without seeking to hide her intent, to the tent where Sir Erec's squires had helped carry their lord. It would have looked suspicious if she'd gone stealthily, so she did not go for stealth. She intended not to hide what she'd done from Bertran, and she already knew he would not object, because she'd vowed to him she was unquestionably his. He would certainly approve of her concern for a vanquished opponent, since he no longer had any cause for jealousy.

She breathed in full relief when she saw Sir Erec was now on his feet, out of his hauberk, wearing his padded tunic. He was nursing a bumped head, but there seemed to be nothing more grievous than that.

Sir Erec instantly dismissed his squires when he glanced upon her.

"Milady?" he asked in a concerned voice.

Alicia spoke urgently.

"It's Godfrey. You need to tell your squires to reassure him as soon as can be. Otherwise… I fear people have started casting suspicious glances. He seemed very distressed when you fell… and he looked as if he might faint."

Sir Erec cursed under his breath.

"The fool!" he muttered. "He may well have been the cause of my last fall. I knew he was fretting over me during the joust, and I could not help but glance at his distress."

He narrowed his eyes at her.

"You are more valiant than he is. After the first joust, I looked upon you to make sure you were well. You did not even bat an eyelid when your husband fell. That is the right way to behave when one's beloved is in a joust. One needn't show fear."

Alicia suppressed a smile. She had been, in fact, mortally afraid for Bertran. Yet she'd known it would serve nothing if she showed her fear. She did not look down upon Haughton for his tender heart.

"Send word to Godfrey somehow! Right now!" she said in haste. "I'm glad you're well. I must go to my husband."

Sir Erec nodded and smiled somewhat begrudgingly.

"His lance hits like a hammer, I'll give him that. Less skill than I have, yet more strength. You should tell him I don't begrudge him his victory. We had a fair fight. It was my own fault my mind was elsewhere."

Alicia cast Erec a hasty smile, and hurried to leave the tent, hoping in the cheering for her husband's victory no one had paid much mind to her. She was reassured when she came upon a crowd of people surrounding her husband, who had yet to shed his hauberk and helmet, as well as the rest of his armour.

"Make way," she called, making her voice unconcerned and letting the joy she felt slip through it. "I need to see my lord."

She glanced upon Sir Bertran in full relief when she could get near him. His posture indicated he had sustained no wound from his earlier fall. Her heart skipped a beat because he looked just as formidable in his full knightly armour as he had looked upon his horse when he'd wielded his lance. He was a valiant knight, and she was proud he was her husband. She had been truly afraid he would get hurt, but now relief and elation were taking hold of her. He was hale. And he had done what his liege had asked of him. All was well then, and she could put her arms around him when they were finally alone, away from the prying eyes of the crowd.

She wanted to speak to her husband, yet she saw King Henry was by his side, beaming.

"A fine beginning for the tournament!" the king was saying. "And it is only the first joust. There'll be the melee the day after tomorrow and we'll have occasion to see even more of your prowess, won't we, Sir Bertran?"

"Yes, my liege," her husband acquiesced.

She caught his glance upon her, and she smiled, a brilliant smile meant to show him the relief she felt that he was safe and sound, and all had gone according to his wishes. He did not return her smile, but Alicia knew he must be weary and still somewhat battle-frenzied. She retreated, knowing they would have the chance to talk at length later when they regained their home. And she steeled herself against ever showing her husband any fear she felt for his safety. She understood why Sir Erec had been angry with Godfrey. A knight had to focus on the task ahead, without any distractions. And this was only the first joust of the tournament. Her husband would face more challenges, and she knew he held his *tourneyer* skills very dear. She did not want to distract him by sharing her fears with him. So she decided to show herself calm and smiling, so she would not be a burden for him in the days ahead.

BERTRAN HAD NEVER THOUGHT that place in his body could ache so fiercely. It was, he understood, the place where his heart was. Yet there shouldn't have been any ache in that side of his body. His flank and hip hurt, from the fall he'd taken when de Jarnac had unhorsed him, yet his heart should be fine. It wasn't though.

She had not come. She had not come running to him when he'd had his victory, and he'd had to stand in the crowd around him, with no sign of his lady wife to rejoice for what he'd done in order to prove himself worthy of her. Instead of Alicia's sweet face, he'd had to put up with a crowd of strangers who did not genuinely care for him. And he did not care for crowds. He cared for his wife, yet his wife had not been there.

He replayed in his head Lady Edith's hurtful words before the joust. They couldn't be true, could they? And even if they were true and his wife still harboured tender feelings for De Jarnac, he had been able to show her, on the jousting field, he was the better man. Hadn't he? Now she would no longer care for her former, vanquished lover.

Bertran chased away these thoughts, disgusted with himself. It was as if he was begging for his wife's regard. He strived to appear unconcerned, and to curve his lips into a victorious smile, as he began to head for the tent where his squires would assist him in the removing of his armour.

From the corner of his eye, he could now perceive Lady Edith casting him mocking glances as she was conferring with a couple of ladies by her side. For some moments, it seemed they were already laughing at him, but he pretended not to notice.

It was in some relief he saw his lady wife was already waiting for him in the tent, standing by as his squires helped him remove his helmet, hauberk, chain mail muffs and chausses, until he was left only in his padded gambeson and braies. Alicia then helped him strip off his gambeson and presented him with a fresh tunic. When Bertran dismissed his squires, he was finally alone with his wife, and he allowed her to embrace and kiss him on the lips passionately, although he still felt very cross with her for not being there when he'd wanted her by his side.

"Where were you?" he asked tersely, when they finally disentangled from each other.

She looked into his eyes levelly.

"I went to Sir Erec's tent," she told him, confirming his fears. "I had to make sure he was not grievously wounded. You know well it is only the proper thing to inquire after a vanquished opponent. I wanted to be gracious."

He nodded, hiding the deep pain that pierced his chest upon the words. Her words were proper. It was indeed the courtly, gracious thing to inquire after a vanquished rival. Yet he knew too well who this vanquished opponent was. She'd once thought to marry Sir Erec. And if one was to believe Lady Edith's hateful words, his wife cared deeply for this man.

Lady Alicia was now smiling at him, and he noted she was not telling him she'd feared for his safety. He recalled his mother, who always tried to hide her anguish and failed, whenever her husband or sons fought other knights for a prize. But all day Lady Alicia had looked calm and composed, and had seemed to harbour no anguish for him whatsoever. Perhaps Lady Alicia did not truly care for him.

He did not know what to say to her at this time, and felt the hollowness of his victory. It seemed he had not vanquished Sir Erec. Not when his wife had sought to inquire after Sir Erec's health before she'd gone to look upon her own husband.

"I am mightily glad this is done and over with," Lady Alicia muttered. "Still, there are more jousts and the melee to be had, and more tournament days ahead of you."

He searched for any kind of anguish in her voice, yet he could discern none. And then his friends burst into the tent, to give him effusive tokens of admiration, and he saw Lady Alicia step aside as they began to talk of the lance charges with him.

The tournament days that followed went on in a sort of daze, and he strived hard not to think upon the pain in his heart or upon his wife. He did well. Yet he was wise enough to let the king's son, Young Henry, rob him of the prize that should have been his. He sensed that Young Henry had more need of the prize than he did, and he also sensed Henry's royal father, while he despised tournaments, was not entirely blind to his eldest son's accomplishments. So he downplayed his own skill in the melee fight, in order to let the young king win. He felt his own triumph was less important than the future of the entire country. Young Henry would be appeased by this prize at least for a while. And perchance his improved humour might lead to a reconciliation with his father.

De Jarnac came in third place for the tournament, having managed to defeat most of his opponents. It was a very close third to his second, and Bertran had already begun to suspect that, like himself, Sir Erec had downplayed his own skill in order to let the young king win.

It was in the last day of the tournament that Sir Erec came to speak to him, holding out his hand. Bertran took the hand that was offered, begrudgingly, because he had naught to reproach his opponent on the field. The fight had been fair and honourable.

"Next time, Sir Bertran," Sir Erec said with an infuriatingly handsome smile. "Next time I swear the outcome of our encounter will be different."

Bertran narrowed his eyes at his rival. He measured him, knowing the fiend was handsome. He'd heard all the ladies at Court were swooning over him. And, unlike his own face, Erec's face was unmarred by a battle scar. It was the first time in his life that Bertran had ever cared about his own appearance. He nearly cursed under his breath. The fault lay entirely with his wife, who still carried a torch for this man.

"I think not. I mean to always be the victor," he growled in response to Sir Erec's teasing tone.

If things had been different, he would have answered Sir Erec's teasing with good humour and a pat on the back, but things were not different.

"Mark my words, if I as much as see you glance again upon my lady wife, I'll have your blood," he added softly, lacing menace inside his voice.

It seemed to him Sir Erec's eyes widened in surprise and he saw him open his mouth. Yet what Sir Erec had meant to say was cut by a call from King Henry who was standing behind them. They both stood to attention, since it was their sovereign who was calling upon them, so Bertran never found out what Sir Erec had meant to say. Besides, he told himself with an angry sneer, he had no wish to know what Erec would have to say.

# CHAPTER 14

During the first days after the tournament, Bertran had been mostly absent from home and he'd spoken little to Alicia when they were alone. He had not touched her at all during those days, but in the beginning she had assumed he was weary after the fighting, and she had decided to be wise and just let him be. She had told herself he would soon become her passionate and mischievous husband again, and the light and laughter were bound to return to his hazel eyes after he let go of his weariness. Yet it had not been so. For two weeks now, Bertran had been behaving coldly towards her. And she'd felt puzzled and hurt by this new behaviour.

It did not help that they were still both tethered to the court. There were days when they barely saw each other. Often, he got back well after midnight, and there was no time to exchange true talk. He often left at dawn, before she roused.

At last it became plain to Alicia that he'd truly changed towards her. Gone was that mischievousness in his gold flecked hazel eyes, gone were the teasing and the lingering caresses. He barely looked at her now, and when he deigned to make love to her, it was as if she were coupling with a stranger. She was, as always, wet for him when he thrust inside her, but he didn't seem to rejoice in her willingness. She'd tried to use sweet words and caresses, but he'd shrugged them away. And she'd tried to talk to him, inquiring if she had offended him somehow. But he'd cut her short whenever she'd tried to confer with him. She'd then, on purpose, behaved discourteously, only to attempt to get some sort of response from him, yet he had not seemed to care about her behaviour.

And today, when at last they were both free from Court to spend their day as they pleased, she'd utterly lost her temper, and she'd started shouting at him in anger, demanding to know why he was treating her with such disdain.

"You'd better hold your tongue, my lady. There's nothing I wish to hear from you at this time," he told her and his voice sounded cold and weary.

Again she tried to get him to tell her why he was acting as if she'd done something wrong.

"Why are you behaving so, my lord? What have I done to deserve this treatment?" she demanded, deciding it was high time to end this strain, which had lingered between them for two weeks.

He said nothing, just stared away from her.

"Is there a woman you've found at Court who pleases you better than I? Is that it?" Alicia asked, resolving to voice the fears, which had been plaguing her ever since he'd become cold towards her.

He gave a short, bitter laugh, but did not answer her. So, was she right? When she'd wed, Alicia had not expected her husband to keep faith with her. Men were fickle, and her father had always considered it his right to bed other women beside her mother, while his wife had kept faith with him. Alicia's own mother had not seemed distressed by it. Men have their urges, she'd told her daughter with an unconcerned shrug. As long as the husband is courteous and does not flaunt his women, doing this quietly, wives have naught to complain about. Her father had been courteous and had behaved affectionately to her mother, yet Alicia had always known there'd been other women.

She took a deep breath, understanding that, unlike her mother, she could never be complacent about it. She didn't want another woman touching her husband. She just wanted him for herself. She loved him. And now he was casting her a bitter, angry glance. Even in his anger, he looked comely, but, she understood, it was not only that he was comely. He was valiant and honourable and level-headed. He could be mischievous and even harsh, yet he'd never been unkind. And until this strange coldness had seized him, she'd begun to think he'd truly grown to care for her. But perhaps he didn't. Perhaps he now cared for some lady love at Court.

"Husband," she spoke in anger, giving him a stormy look of her own. "Tell me what it is. Let us talk. Perchance you're cold to me because you've found another?"

"I wish it were so," he told her harshly. "That way I wouldn't be the only one who's faithless in this marriage."

Blood rose within her temples. Did he think her faithless?

"Have I ever given you cause to think I've been unfaithful?" she asked in an indignant voice.

He was calling her honour into question, and she would not stand for it. She might love him, but she would not let him treat her with disdain. She'd been loyal and true to him and had tried to be a good wife. It angered her that he could think she was otherwise, and her eyes blazed when she looked upon him.

"I shall not stand for hurtful words, husband! I have never been faithless! You need to take back what you've just uttered!"

Again, he laughed bitterly.

"Maybe not in deed, but I'm certain you're faithless in thought. You dream of the fop, Erec de Jarnac. I'm certain you think of him whenever I thrust inside you. It was, after all, him you wished to marry."

She stared at him. Was that why he'd been so cold and bitter to her? Did he still think she cared for Erec? Hadn't he been able by now to tell how she burnt for him when she was in his arms? Hadn't her loving behaviour to him been proof enough? It seemed incomprehensible. So Bertran's coldness to her had not been prompted by the love for another, but by sheer jealousy. She felt blazingly angry with him for doubting her so, yet she attempted to let go of her anger, because her love burnt brighter than her anger. His words meant he had not broken faith with her, and things could be mended between them.

She opened her mouth to set him at ease.

"I…"

He did not let her finish.

"Don't speak to me if you mean to tell me a lie. I could not bear it," he told her between gritted teeth.

She stared at him in wonder. He was furious with her. And it seemed his fury went deeper than mere offence that she'd dishonoured him. The anguished look he was casting her now meant he cared for more than that. And, suddenly, it was plain. He'd come to love her – just as she'd come to love him. She cast him a brilliant smile, and he scowled at her darkly. Of course, he was still furious with her, but she couldn't bring herself to feel any more anger towards him. He was furious with her because he loved her. What had Master Reed's wife said? That lovemaking after a harsh punishment felt more wondrous than anything in this world. That the bond of love felt truer and deeper after chastisement and reconciliation had taken place.

"Why don't you punish me if you think I did wrong? You've always believed it is within your rights to do so," she said softly.

These past weeks, she'd tried to provoke him to spank her, thinking a spanking might bring a closeness, which would mend the rift between them. So, there had been times when she'd spoken to him more than defiantly, hoping he would chastise her for it. But it had been to no avail. Bertran had not seemed to care about her defiance.

He now cast her a wilting look.

"I recall the last time I spanked you. I recall your soaking wet cunt and your moans of rapture. Do you think me so feeble-minded? You believe I don't know such a punishment will always seem a reward to you?"

"You could punish me hard. Mercilessly," she offered, thinking a punishment might make him let go of his misplaced anger towards her. By spanking her, he might let go of his resentment, and then, once he saw her chastened and sobbing, he would make deep love to her, and all the mistrust he'd harboured would melt away. After he'd spent the blaze of his passion, he would be prepared to see reason and truly listen to what she had to say.

He shook his head tiredly.

"No," he said in a terse voice.

He stormed out of the room, without giving her the chance to call after him. Alicia heaved a deep sigh. What could she do to make him understand there was no one else she cared for? No one but him? She resolved to make him listen when he returned. And she resolved to tell him of her love. Plainly so. But would he believe her? He didn't seem to trust her at all, which she could not understand. She'd never given him cause for mistrust. Never.

She spent the rest of her morning in turmoil. When a serving girl called to her to come down, her heart started beating in anticipation, thinking her husband had returned home and she would have the chance to reason with him. She resolved to make him listen at all costs, even if she had to shake him. She looked in disappointment upon the visitor standing in the Hall. It was her father, gazing at her with a smile on his face.

Alicia heaved a deep sigh, knowing her father had come to take his leave of her. He would be heading back home, since his rift with Henry seemed to have been miraculously mended. Alicia had fully begun to suspect he was now on Henry's side, and was only leading Eleanor to believe she still had his allegiance. She led him to the solar, and called for refreshments, knowing the words that needed to be spoken between father and daughter had waited long enough.

BERTRAN FELT his heart burn in his chest, as he gazed upon the gelatinous waters of the Thames. For the past hour, he'd been walking the city like mad, trying to still the throbbing pain in his heart. She'd not denied it, had she? She'd not denied that she still carried a torch for Erec de Jarnac.

He raked a hand through his hair, thinking, like so many times before, that his wife was not truly to blame for it. He couldn't reproach her, could he? She'd plainly rejected his suit. And she had probably not broken faith with him. There had been little chance for her to be alone for long with De Jarnac, except for stolen moments at Court, which could be only very brief, as he'd made sure of her whereabouts when she was there. He'd conferred with the serving men who usually accompanied her, and he'd found there had been no impropriety. The lady Alicia, the men had reported, spent most of her time engaged in her various duties and left the house only to go to Court or Mass, or walk through the market in full view. At night she always waited for her husband to come home from Court as she usually arrived before him, and that was all.

Still, Bertran recalled only too well the look in his wife's eyes when she'd told him she'd spoken to Sir Erec after the joust, and he recalled well her loud cry when he'd unhorsed the fop. At the time he'd heard her voice cry out, he'd foolishly believed she'd been truly cheering for him. But he'd perceived her face was distracted and not joyful at all, when he'd looked at her from the tournament field. Besides, she had not been there to embrace him when he'd had his triumph, and she had seemed flustered when at last she'd come to look upon him. He recalled all of Lady Edith's malicious words, which still cut into him like poisonous splinters. After the joust hadn't Alicia gone to Erec first, caring less that her husband was the victor and more that Sir Erec might be wounded? It was only too plain whom she truly cared for.

He stared at the water, pulling his cloak to wrap himself with it and feeling chilled, although the weather was warm and mild. Alicia did not love him. She loved another, and perhaps it would always be so. While he… he loved her. He smiled bitterly, understanding he could no longer disguise it to himself. He'd tried to tell himself he was incensed because he was a wronged husband. But it was not so, was it? He'd been able to perceive the truth in her eyes today when she'd spoken. She had not wronged him. She'd even come to his bed a maiden, and had not broken faith with him since they'd spoken their wedding vows. It was only that she loved another. And it tore his heart out of his chest to think upon it.

Dejectedly, he started dragging his feet back home. Alicia was not to blame, and did not deserve his scorn. He only had himself to blame for it. He loved her, when she could not love him in return. His hounds greeted him back, wagging their tails and trailing after him when he finally stepped inside the Hall. He looked around him, noting the changes Alicia had brought to his home. It had started looking like a home now. Even if she had her own tedious duties at Court, she'd been diligently working for his comfort, and he'd never even found a word of praise for her efforts. She had been trying to be a good and true wife to him, although her heart belonged to another. Instead of seeing that, he'd treated her with disdain.

"Where is your mistress?" he asked a serving girl who was passing by, busy at her chores.

"She's in the solar with the guest, my lord," the girl, a new servant Alicia had employed, told him with a small curtsy.

Guest? What guest? Bertran found himself storming up the stairs, thinking perhaps Erec de Jarnac had decided to come to call upon the woman he loved. He paused in front of the door of the solar, rubbing his temples tiredly. He was behaving like a fool. Of course, De Jarnac would not call upon their house in broad daylight, after Bertran had made it plain he knew of his feelings for Alicia. De Jarnac may dress like a fop, but he was not a fool. Alicia was probably entertaining a different guest. Bertran prepared to enter the solar and greet their guest, when the sound of angry voices was heard from behind the door.

Alicia's voice was incensed.

"I do not understand you! Now you behave as if nothing untoward has happened, as if all along you were in favour of the match, and I was the only one against it!"

Another voice followed, placating, which Bertran recognised after a while as belonging to Lord de Lancres.

"Come, come, daughter, I can see the way you're acting around the bastard. I know you well enough to see you're besotted with him. The match has proved a success, in spite of our misgivings, so why are you complaining?"

"I'm not complaining of the match! I'm complaining of your behaviour! You wrote the letter in *my* name! You spewed insults against the De Mornes in a letter that bore my name, so if the king decided to take offence, *I* would be the one to take the blame! I was humiliated in front of the entire Court and you stood by! You didn't even have the decency to tell me I'd been summoned to Court for a chastisement!"

There was a pause before Lord de Lancres spoke.

"What could I have done? Eleanor was not inclined to offer protection. The king had taken offense, and he would have been incensed if he'd found out I'd been responsible. You know he covets what's mine, he covets my wealth and lands…"

"You should have thought of that before you wrote the letter!"

"But I was doing only what we agreed upon. You said Fitz-Rolf was unsuitable, beneath you in rank and wealth…"

"Yes, I did, but not because he was born a bastard! I did not look down upon him because of it, knowing he was a worthy knight. I merely weighed his suit against that of Sir Erec. Sir Erec's name is more ancient and his estates are vaster! He seemed like an amiable man and I was already acquainted with him. Sir Erec seemed like a reasonable choice. I trusted you would write a gracious letter of rejection to Sir Bertran. *Gracious*! Instead, you took the opportunity to insult him and his family!"

"I got angered. I got angered by the De Mornes' presumptuousness and by the royal favour they'd gained. I knew too well what Henry was doing. He was using them in order to undermine my authority! He was using them in his feud with Eleanor!"

"But instead of talking to me of it, honourably and honestly, you chose to act behind my back, knowing I would be the one to get the blame for your insults if the king decided to act!"

Silence fell, before Lord de Lancres said, "Please, daughter, I will not have us part in anger. I was wrong, but things have not turned out for the worst, have they? I've reconciled myself with it, and I've decided to start supporting the king, as I can see the queen is not going to be the victor. Besides, Henry now seems more favourably disposed towards me, now that you've wed the man of his choice. And you're happy with your match, aren't you?"

"Aye, I am happy with the match. It turns out Sir Bertran was indeed the better choice. But that is beside the point and you know it. You just stood by and let me take the blame! And Bertran and his family still believe me guilty!"

Bertran had heard enough. He flung the door open, as deep relief coursed through his veins.

"De Lancres," he said, not bothering to offer a courteous greeting.

Lord de Lancres looked flustered, but attempted to plaster an amiable smile on his face.

"I was just talking to my daughter, saying that…"

"I know too well what you were saying. I heard it all."

De Lancres blanched.

"I… The king… You wouldn't speak to the king about it, would you? We are related now, come to think of it, and no longer on opposite sides."

Bertran gave a short laugh.

"You're lucky Lady Alicia still calls you her father. Otherwise, I would have challenged you."

Alicia came to place a placating hand on his shoulder.

"Just leave him be, husband. There's no need the king find out what has occurred."

De Lancres was still staring at Bertran. His hands had closed around the back of the chair behind which he was standing. His knuckles were white and his eyes shone with fear.

Bertran turned his head in disgust. He spoke only to his wife.

"Since you're asking it of me, I will keep silent. But I want him gone from my house. He's not fit to look upon you, not after the cowardly, treacherous way he's treated you!"

De Lancres didn't wait for his daughter to reply.

"I shall take my leave of you then, daughter, wishing you all the happiness in this new marriage!" he said hurriedly, then beat a hasty retreat.

Bertran stared after him in wonder.

"Has he always been like that, your father? Fickle and cowardly?"

Alicia heaved a sigh.

"Yes, I suppose he has, though I was often too blind to perceive it. He is my father, you see."

Bertran nodded. He now understood what life must have been for her, and that people misjudged her. They thought her an arrogant woman who kept her father under her thumb, not perceiving her father was a weak, cowardly man, and she'd had no one to rely upon apart from herself. She must have been the one to shoulder the full burden of their estates, with no help from her irresponsible parent. She was a strong, decisive woman because she'd had to be so. And Bertran found he preferred to have such a strong, decisive woman by his side, instead of a meek, subservient wife. She would always look to their family's interests and fiercely protect them. His mother had been right in her choice. Lady Alicia was a good match for him, and it was not so because she was a great heiress. It was so because she was the woman she was.

"Did you hear everything?" Lady Alicia asked.

He nodded, and she cast him a rueful smile.

"So, now you know. I did not mean to offend you. It is not my way. I'd trusted my father would send a gracious rejection, because it was the honourable thing to do. I never dreamt he would be so foolish or use my name to show his support of Eleanor."

She then added in a warm voice, taking his hand in hers.

"I've never looked down upon what you are. And now that we're wed I've come to see how wrong I was. You're a better choice than Sir Erec was. Sir Erec... We would never have suited. And there's no attachment between Sir Erec and me."

Bertran raked a hand through his hair, understanding his searing jealousy had blinded him to what had been in front of him. Alicia had come to care for him – it was plain in the way she'd acted, and in all those gestures of affection she'd tried to make when he'd behaved coldly to her. Instead of drawing away when faced with his churlishness, she'd tried to mend the rift between them. And he'd rejected her. He had behaved wretch-edly. He now recalled how hard he'd spanked her in front of all the court to see. He recalled the humiliation and grief he'd caused her. A humiliation she'd borne with dignity, though she'd not been guilty of anything.

"So, the day of our wedding, I spanked you for nothing!" he said in a dejected voice.

She opened her mouth to speak, but he did not let her.

"You bore it all, and you didn't protest! Why?" he asked incredulously.

She heaved a sigh.

"It would have been to no avail. No one would have believed me, and it would have made me look cowardly. Besides, it would have dishonoured my father…"

"He'd already dishonoured himself!"

"You're right. But you know as well as I do that King Henry would have been incensed. Who knows what he would have done? Don't you think he'd have used the opportunity to seize our lands? Eleanor couldn't help, so I had no choice. Besides, you were right, you said a sore bottom and bruised pride can easily heal."

He looked at her pointedly.

"And did they?" he asked in a gentle voice.

She nodded, with a smile.

"Aye. They did."

SHE WAS SPEAKING THE TRUTH, and now, smiling to herself, she realised something of great importance. If it hadn't been for that spanking, Bertran and she would never have wed. She now saw that spanking not as a humiliating story to be forgotten at all costs, but as a story she and her husband would fondly remember during the years they had ahead of them. Strangely, what had started as deep humiliation had ended up as a fond memory. A burning one, for sure, but a fond memory, nevertheless.

"Forgive me," Bertran suddenly told her, and the words rang humble.

"There's nothing to forgive!" she said, knowing he had his own pride, and hadn't spoken the words lightly.

He shook his head, perusing her with his fine hazel eyes.

"But there is. You bore it all patiently, with barely a word of complaint. And you've been a good wife, while I haven't been a good husband. I doubted you. I was cross and ill-tempered and unfair…"

She opened her mouth to stop him, but he went on.

"And now I'm humbly begging your forgiveness, because this is what I should do. You must know you already have my heart, my lady. It is yours to do with what you please."

He bent his knee, bowing his head in a humble gesture of obeisance.

"Rise, sir knight," Alicia told him, smiling. "There's no need to serve penance, and nothing you did which cannot be undone."

He did as she'd bid him, coming to take her in his arms.

"I love thee true," he said softly.

"And so do I," she acquiesced in an ardent voice.

There was kissing, and then more than kissing. Much more. Later, in their chamber, as Alicia came to lie sated in her husband's strong arms, she decided she'd gotten her wish. She'd gotten a husband who was suitable for her. He might not be the biddable man she'd wished for at first, but she'd come to see a biddable man wouldn't have suited her at all.

"You did promise to be a dutiful husband," she whispered softly in his ear, after she'd trailed teasing kisses on his neck and chest.

"I did. And it is a promise I intend to keep."

"I shall strive to be a dutiful wife, in return. And I assume I shall be spanked whenever I don't act like a dutiful wife," she said lazily.

He laughed.

"No."

She sat up with a frown.

"No?"

He grinned at her, now lightly toying with her nipple.

"Of course not. That won't be a punishment at all. You enjoy it far too much. Besides…"

"Yes?" she asked, her breathing now laboured and her sex already tingling due to what his clever fingers were doing to her breast.

"I also enjoy it far too much," he said softly, then took her nipple in his mouth.

## CHAPTER 15

$S$ ometime later, when they'd at last finished what they had started, Alicia heaved a deep sigh, which was both sated and vexed. So her husband had resolved there'd be no more spankings…

"Then you won't ever discipline me again?" she asked in some disappointment.

"You might be haughty and fierce at times, but you're true and loyal. You're a level-headed woman, who doesn't act foolishly. I've come to see that. You're a woman who can be reasoned with," he told her in a serious voice. "I never disciplined my first wife, because there was no need to. And I don't think I'll have true cause to discipline you."

She sighed, happy he'd come to see her worth, but dejected he would not spank her again. She'd come to crave that strange sensation where pleasure mingled with pain, where rapture mingled with embarrassment.

"Of course," he added, with teasing in his voice. "That doesn't mean I won't spank you if you shamelessly ask for it. Since I promised to be a dutiful husband, I shall strive to take care of my lady wife's needs. I daresay my lady wife needs to be spanked at times, when naughty thoughts come to her head."

Her heart skipped a beat.

"Husband," she muttered. "I think I have some very naughty thoughts in my head right now."

"Oh, so you wish me to spank those naughty thoughts out of you?" her husband asked, pulling her to him, and beginning to rub her bare bottom in slow, tantalizing circles.

Alicia's sex filled with molten heat, in anticipation of what would follow.

"Be careful what you wish for, my lady. Because I've come to like to spank soundly, just like a stern, dutiful husband should," he told her in a soft voice.

"I wouldn't wish it otherwise," she countered.

A while later, as she lay across his lap, bare-assed and already soundly spanked, Alicia was starting to feel rather sorry for herself and for her scorched behind. She'd forgotten how large her husband's hand was, and how well it could warm her bottom. He had promised he'd be stern, hadn't he? And he had been stern indeed. The pain in her bottom was already fierce, and made her regret she'd dared him to spank her. Yet, her sex was wet and pulsing. She could feel his hard cock pressing against her as she lay face down over his lap.

She braced herself for the next spank, which seemed to be tarrying. The fiend now meant to torture her, by prolonging her wait. Yet, instead of a spank, Alicia felt Bertran's hand parting her wet folds. His finger slid in and out of her slick sheath, then rubbed the inflamed kernel of her womanhood. Alicia nearly peaked. But the fiend wouldn't let her find her release. Instead, he withdrew his finger, now beginning to rub her scorched bottom with his large hand that had earlier spanked her so soundly. Strange that a large hand like his could be both merciful and merciless at the same time. His ministrations made Alicia whimper in both pleasure and pain.

When at last he let her off his lap, Alicia thought he would make love to her, and she wiped her tears, looking at him in eager anticipation. Instead, he told her calmly he wasn't quite done with her. Alicia did so with a frown, debating within herself whether to argue with him or not. She wanted him to make love to her, because her sex was pulsing with the need for him. She opened her mouth to tell him so, beginning to rub her bottom through her skirts, because her bottom was now too tender to bear the touch of her clothes. It already smarted, and his large hand had covered all of it quite thoroughly. She had no doubt it was glowing red now.

"Did I say you were allowed to rub your chastened bottom, my lady?" he asked her softly.

She shook her head, as an ignoble stab of rapture pierced her sex. So, he was not done toying with her, was he?

He sat himself on the bed, patting his lap and calling in a voice that held a mixture of sternness and teasing.

"Naughty wives get spanked again for rubbing their naughty bottoms."

Alicia rolled her eyes, but nevertheless obeyed his command. She had asked for this, hadn't she?

He settled her over his knees, making quick work of hoisting her skirts.

"I told you to be careful what you wish for, my lady," he told her, lightly brushing his fingers over her smarting buttocks.

He didn't give her a chance to answer, but proceeded to spank her as mercilessly as he had before, now also peppering her upper thighs, which he hadn't attended to in his previous spanking. Alicia soon found herself in tears, and nearly begged him to stop. The spanking was almost as hard as the one he'd delivered when they'd first met, yet not as hard. Or was it just as hard as that first punishment? She didn't have time to think. His first spanks had been slow and methodical, with long pauses between them. The ones he'd begun to deliver now were far more rapid, and they stung like a thousand hornets. The pain was almost excruciating. What had possessed her to ask for a spanking? She only had herself to blame for it, and for the sorry state of her behind. But all coherent thought was robbed from her when he delivered his next smack right on her blazing red sit spot. This was followed by several more rapid spanks right on the same abused spot.

When the large punishing hand stopped, Alicia breathed a sigh of relief, thinking the chastisement was finally done and time had come for soothing. Her husband spat into his palm, and proceeded to rub her bottom just as he'd done the first time. Yet now his palm was wet. This wet palm upon her scorched behind felt like a balm, the coolness of it soothing her seared skin and sending tingles through her entire body that made her curl her toes and arch her back in rapture. After the heat of the spanking, this felt like bliss. Her husband chuckled when he heard her moan, but Alicia soon had cause to find out he wasn't quite done with her. The caressing hand became punishing again, and the swats he landed upon her now wet bottom seemed to hurt a hundred times more than the ones before. Yet she did not have time to protest her pain, as suddenly the hand that had been punishing became caressing again. One of its fingers found anew the hidden part of her sex he'd come to fondly call her little rose thorn and stroked it even more tantalizingly than before. This time she succumbed to the pleasure of it, crying out her deep rapture, as the fierce burn in her bottom and the excruciating pleasure in her sheath mingled within her.

She was both smiling and crying when her punisher straightened her skirts and let her off his lap, and her heart was thumping wildly. The look in his fine hazel eyes, and the stiff cock she'd felt pressing against her, and that she now fully perceived when he rose from the bed, told her that he was revelling in this just as much as she did. Was he already done with her, or would he give her more? She didn't feel ready for more, and yet… She broadened her smile within herself, looking upon her husband in anticipation. So, what did he have in store for her next?

The End

R. R. VANE

I discovered romance in a shop which sold used books when I was a teen and I have been writing romance novels in my head ever since. My first ever draft was a medieval romance with a gray-eyed knight, and I still want to finish it one day. For me writing is a dream come true and I always try to stay true to my dreams. So I write historical/paranormal/fantasy romance. My first book (*A Deep Dark Call,* published as Rose Vane) is a Gothic romance set in nineteenth-century Romania. *A Stern Knight for My Lady* is the first medieval romance I ever published.

Visit her website here:
https://rosevane.com/

Don't miss these exciting titles by R. R. Vane and Blushing Books!

A Stern Night for My Lady

# BLUSHING BOOKS

Blushing Books is the oldest eBook publisher on the web. We've been running websites that publish steamy romance and erotica since 1999, and we have been selling eBooks since 2003. We have free and promotional offerings that change weekly, so please do visit us at http://www.blushingbooks.com/free.

# BLUSHING BOOKS NEWSLETTER

Please join the Blushing Books newsletter
to receive updates & special promotional offers.
You can also join by using your mobile phone:
Just text BLUSHING to 22828.

Every month, one new sign up via text messaging will receive a
$25.00 Amazon gift card, so sign up today!